Hope you enjoy

A MATTER OF DARK

love

A MATTER OF DARK

GARETH WILES

Matador
9 Priory Business Park
Kibworth Beauchamp
Leicestershire LE8 0RX, UK
Tel: (+44) 116 279 2299
Fax: (+44) 116 279 2277
Email: books@troubador.co.uk
Web: www.troubador.co.uk/matador

ISBN 978 1780884 875

British Library Cataloguing in Publication Data.
A catalogue record for this book is available from the British Library.

Typeset in 11pt Book Antiqua by Troubador Publishing Ltd, Leicester, UK

Matador is an imprint of Troubador Publishing Ltd

Printed and bound in the UK by TJ International, Padstow, Cornwall

For You

7PM NEWS: TONIGHT

'Tonight at 10, Peter Smith will commit suicide live on TV and you, the viewers at home, can vote for which method he uses. Joining us from outside the studio where the event is to start broadcasting at 9 is suicide prevention worker Felicity Wood and on the sofa pro-suicide campaigner, and self-confessed Peter Smith fan and follower, Neville Jeffries. Felicity, Neville - thanks.'

'Richard, this is clearly a crass stunt designed to raise Mr Smith's profile. He's a Z-list pseudo-religious figure clamouring for exposure who has about as much intention of committing suicide as me,' Felicity begins.

'Well your husband did,' Neville snorts back at her.

'You, Mr Jeffries, are as bad as Mr Smith. Neither of you understand the awful, sensitive and heart-wrenching nature of suicide and broadcasting such a stunt, because that is all it is, a stunt, is an absolute disgrace. You are treating suicide like entertainment. It's just a joke to you. I urge everybody to change channel and boycott the transmission of this programme.'

Neville laughs.

'Neville?' Newsman Richard Hart asks his guest in the studio.

'No, no, not true at all, Richard. For the real reason behind Peter's stunt, er, decision, we must look more closely at the man himself. His work allows us a portal into the mind of a genius - a tortured genius - who we must all look up to.'

'Rubbish,' Felicity shouts.

'Please, let me finish. Here is a man opening his heart to the world one last time as he takes the decision to leave us by his own hand to go on to higher things - higher plains of existence. And, let me point out, Felicity, that Peter has always shunned publicity. This will mark his first, and last, public appearance.'

'By his own hand? Neville, may I remind you that there will be a phone-in giving viewers the opportunity to vote for which method Mr Smith uses. What sort of a message does that send out?'

'Look, it's after the watershed, what's the problem?' Neville replies nonchalantly.

'Felicity,' Richard asks, scratching his chin with a pen, 'do you think this will spark copycat suicides, perhaps on the internet?'

'I do, yes. This is a dark day for suicide prevention.'

'Don't make me laugh,' Neville cuts in, 'there have already been plenty of online videos of people killing themselves. That's nothing new. That's like saying computer games invented knife crime or something. If anything, this *RAISES* the profile of your cause, Felicity.'

'How does asking viewers to phone-in and vote for how Mr Smith commits suicide help prevent suicide?'

'Isn't one of the options to *NOT* do it?' Richard asks, checking the papers on his desk.

'Yes, Richard, exactly!' Neville throws his arms in the air.

'So surely the general public will opt for that?' Richard continues.

'The opinion polls have already suggested that the people most likely to actually pick up their phones and vote will opt for the most horrific method. We're not talking about little old ladies here, this show is pandering to a minority of sick, sick people - a minority Mr Jeffries belongs to.'

'Oh come on. This is Peter's life, he can do what he wants with it. He's taking control,' Neville shouts back.

'Neville,' Richard interjects, 'what is your reaction to the stats that show ad revenue for this event is far higher than a show normally in this time slot, and that Peter's book has seen a surge in sales?'

'This is THE event of the year, perhaps of the decade... or even the whole of human existence. It is the ultimate reality TV show. Have you ever read his book?'

'No.'

'I AM DEAD is the masterpiece of the 21st century - of any century.'

'Conversely, it could also be described as a badly-written flop that most of us hadn't even heard of prior to the announcement of this broadcast,' Richard adds.

'No, no, that's all wrong. It is beyond criticism.'

'You, Mr Jefferies, are little more than an obsessed fan - one of the very few Mr Smith actually has, might I add,' Felicity chirps. 'This is likely little more than a promotional effort on Mr Smith's part for his cult in Harnlan.'

'We, his supporters, intend to bring it to the masses as soon as possible in order to deliver his word,' Neville roars, waving his fist.

'Deliver his word? Are you suggesting Mr Smith is some sort of religious deity, Mr Jefferies?'

'He WILL rise again! You will ALL bow down to his whim!' Neville calls out, looking directly into the camera, before giggling.

'I can see tensions are running high at the moment.' Richard turns back to face the camera. 'The live suicide of Peter Smith, starting at 9 tonight, has split opinion on both sides of the suicide debate. Some say it is the lowest form of reality show we have yet experienced in this country, with a phone vote giving viewers the option to choose which method Peter uses as proof of this. Others say this is a step forward in promoting suicide as a legitimate way out after the controversial legalising of assisted dying just weeks ago. Earlier we spoke to the Prime Minister for his reaction to the impending broadcast.'

PM'S OPINION:

'Look, this is not a debate about whether or not we should have legalised assisted dying, this is a debate about one man's television stunt. I truly believe he has no intention whatsoever of going through with it, no matter what the result of this phone vote is.'

'Do you intend to call for the show to be taken off the air and not broadcast?'

'That is not in my power. The channel executives are in charge of what they broadcast, not me. They have the freedom to broadcast whatever they and their regulators deem worthy.'

'Do you deem it worthy?'

'That is not what we're discussing here.'

'But do you?'

'As I say, it doesn't matter what my personal opinion on the matter is, what's really at stake here is-'

Richard interrupts: 'Isn't channel executive Helen O'Sullivan a cousin of yours?'

'I have nothing further to say on the matter.'

BACK IN THE STUDIO:

'In other news, a man shot dead his wife and two young daughters today before taking his own life in a fire at their idyllic countryside home. It is understood he had run into financial difficulty after being made redundant two months ago. Kanak Ollam is at the scene...'

A SPAYED OF CATNAPPINGS

(TEN YEARS AGO)

ONE

Peter Smith, having been rescued by a farmer in a field following the attempt on his life by police officer Jim, alerted the authorities as to what had happened. Jim had simply run him down, unprovoked, dragged him into the field and tried to set him on fire. Fate had conspired against Jim, for a bull had appeared and done him in before he could do Peter in. Jim's body, having been torn to shreds by the bull, was eventually collected and pieced back together for his relatives to dispose of at their discretion. It was a rather upsetting and perplexing affair. Two officers were dead. First David, and then Jim. What the others didn't know, of course, was that Jim had been responsible for David's death and this was to forever remain hidden from them. Why he had flipped and tried to kill Peter also remained just from their grasp. We were, to describe this whole thing correctly, nearing the end. However, there was still some distance to travel as Stephen Noble and Darren Aubrey yet remained to fulfil Reaping Icon's request. They were to kill Peter. The others had failed. And, of course, there was to be revealed the purpose of all this. Here is where we continue, and shortly conclude, this affair.

Ruby and Arthur were sitting watching TV one morning when Katie suddenly shouted from upstairs:

'Mum!' But she was ignored. Arthur checked his watch on the hand resting on his beer belly as Ruby turned the volume up. 'MUM!' she repeated, louder.

'Keep your voice down,' Ruby shouted back, keeping her eyes on the TV, 'we're trying to watch the telly.'

'There's no toilet paper.'

'What do you want me to do about it, come up there and lick your arse clean?' she screeched back in distress, pulling at the mound of greying red curls atop her head.

'Fine, I'll use your flannel.'

Katie marched into TARRANT'S, the local shop just around the corner from Myrtle Mews. It was a convenience to go there, being as it was a convenience store - though the prices were rather high. That was, perhaps, why people had begun to shop at the new cheaper, and larger, LENNON'S just a bit further down the road. Nevertheless, Katie needed the convenience of easy access to toilet rolls and that was, to put it simply, why she was now in TARRANT'S. The extra few metres to LENNON'S were an inconvenience when you were in quick need of toilet paper. However, looking around, she could not see any toilet rolls on display. The hunched redhead stepped up to the counter and was greeted by Emma, who appeared from behind a curtain which led into the back store room.

'Katie! What are you doing here?' she asked her bewildered friend.

'Oh, I just popped in for some toilet paper. More to the point, what are YOU doing here?'

'I work here, remember,' said the attractive brunette, now in her eighteenth year.

'I don't remember, you never told me.'

Sharon, a slim and short woman in her late thirties, suddenly appeared from within one of the aisles. 'Hello sunshine!' she beamed at Katie, a bizarre open-mouthed grin displaying the first signs of smoking-related gum disease.

'Sharon, did you know about Emma working here?'

'Common news, Katie,' Sharon replied, again in a high-pitched squeal, 'everyone knows. Universal knowledge, darlin'.'

'Well I didn't,' Katie sulked. 'I'm the only one without a job now.'

'What about lover boy Alex?' Sharon giggled, leaning in and jabbing Katie with her sharp index finger. Perhaps she had meant it as a friendly poke. Katie edged away, keen not to inhale any of Sharon's cigarette breath. 'He's a professional bum. Oh, and WHAT a bum.'

'No he's not! He works in LENNON'S down the road.'

'Ah yeah, the new competition for TARRANT'S! Oh the excitement, the thrills! My guess is,' and she leant back in towards Katie again, lowering her voice, 'Tarrant will bump Lennon off.' She winked. 'Some say it was him who killed Timothy, not Michelle.' Suddenly she waved a box of eggs in Katie's face and burst into laughter. 'Anyway, I better be off! Only popped in for some eggs for dear old Gerty and look what happens, you plebs keep me talkin'. Tut tut!' With this, and a perplexed look from both Katie and Emma, Sharon promptly made her exit.

Katie turned to Emma, asking: 'Did she pay for those?'

'Damn! That's what I keep forgetting with all these customers.'

Katie looked around the shop for said customers. It was empty. Tarrant - the eponymous obese middle-aged proprietor of the shop - struggled from behind the loosely-draped curtain and came to stand next to Emma. His stomach came to rest on the counter as his breath wheezed for mercy.

'Emma, I wonder if you could go in the back room and sort out those toilet rolls for me?' he gasped.

'Oh, that's what I came in for,' Katie interjected.

'I know,' Tarrant responded, his eyes focused on her legs.

'O…kay then,' was Katie's uneasy acceptance of this.

Tarrant pulled a pen from his tight trouser pocket and casually dropped it on the floor in front of Emma.

'Oh, I'll get that, Sir,' she responded, bending down to pick the pen up. Tarrant's eyes fixed on her bum, his tongue protruding somewhat. 'Here we are,' Emma said as she passed the pen back to her boss. He took it from her, making sure to touch her fingers, before slipping it back in his pocket as his eyes rolled to the back of his head.

'The toilet rolls,' he nudged, flicking his eyes towards the back room.

'Oh, right. Yes, sorry.' She disappeared behind the curtain.

'Hey, you,' Katie shot at him.

'I know you,' he shot back with even more venom than she. 'Get out of my shop, you red-haired weasel.'

'No! How dare you! Are you some kind of pervert or something?'

'I beg your pardon?'

'I saw the way you were dribbling over my friend's bottom.'

'Run along, little girl,' Tarrant sighed, opening a magazine on the counter and flicking through it, 'let the adults get on with their work.' He burped.

'I'm watching you,' Katie carried on, making her way to the exit.

'Oh, I'm shuddering. What you gonna do, send your lout of a father round?'

'You can shove your toilet rolls up your big fat backside, I'm going to *LENNON'S* instead.' She stormed out, just as Gerty stormed in in her wheelchair, quickly followed by Sharon. The old bag, grabbing hold of the eggs off her lap, screamed at Sharon:

'I told you to get a dozen, not half a dozen.' She threw the box of eggs onto the floor.

'What seems to be the problem here?' Tarrant questioned nonchalantly.

'Well, I sent this dim-witted misfit round to fetch me home a dozen eggs - what does she bring back but a mere half that amount!' Gerty seethed.

'Would these half a dozen eggs you refer to be the ones that now grace my freshly moped shop floor?'

'I want a dozen eggs!' Gerty continued to screech.

'Well why did you chuck those on the floor you stupid old hag? Surely you could have just bought another box,' Tarrant yelled back.

'Certainly not! That would never do. Now, you ridiculously fat oaf, I want a full refund on those damaged eggs you tried to palm off on me, and a set of a dozen fresh eggs, free of charge, for the stress and trauma your sorry excuse of a shop has caused me.'

'Go home you dotty old bat whilst you still can,' Tarrant continued.

'Am I to infer from that statement that you intend me ill should I not return forthwith?' Gerty, horrified, howled. She wheeled herself closer to the man, catching sight of his hands. 'My word, should you really be serving customers with those filthy nails?'

Katie made her way up the Myrtle Mews cul-de-sac and arrived at the bottom of her driveway. She looked around the street, sighing, before walking to her back door and entering the kitchen. In the street behind her a large lorry began reversing, eventually coming to a stop outside Timothy's old house. Intrigued, Ruby stepped outside for a better look. Arthur joined her, his arms folded, a yawn seizing his jaw. The lorry driver rolled out, slamming his door shut, and ambled to the back where he pressed a large button. The back shutter on the lorry rose, revealing what appeared to be a living room inside. A family were sitting on a sofa and armchairs, with a dining table in front of them. The rest of their worldly goods sat behind them, ready to be unloaded into their new home. The mother, a near twin for Ruby if ever one could be sought, had been given the name Dorothy, and presumably had no issue with the label. Her children, the sixteen-year-old daughter Martha, and eighteen-year-old son Oliver, were the first to jump out of the back of the lorry. Martha, a little tubby like her mother, was not unattractive. In fact, it did not do to stare too long at her big, deep green eyes as it could prove fatal. Oliver was slim, scarily so, and even a little hunched. His long hair - which he continuously flicked about and jostled with - helped to hide this early sign of back trouble. Dorothy joined her children outside in the street, turning back to see her husband Colin, positioned on an armchair, deeply lost in the fishing magazine he was reading. Colin, too, could have been Arthur's long-lost twin. Balding, slightly short and with a little rounded belly, he was the epitome of middle-aged male achievement.

'We've arrived!' Martha exclaimed, catching a brief glimpse around the street.

'You coming, Colin?' Dorothy questioned her husband, seemingly without malice, as Ruby, Arthur and Katie approached.

'What?' Colin called back, his eyes leaving the magazine just long enough to realise the lorry door was open. He edged forward in his chair, continuing to read the magazine, as he attempted to stand up. He grimaced and groaned, appearing to have a bit of back trouble.

'Don't you start complaining about your back! We've got all this rubbish to carry into the new house.'

His response? A yawn.

'Hiya! Are you moving in?' Katie asked the gathering.

'That's right,' Dorothy responded, eyes still fixed on Colin. Oliver, flicking his hair from his face, eyed Katie up and down with a sly grin. 'I'm Mrs Dodd,' Dorothy continued, turning and holding her hand out at Katie.

'Mrs Dodd?' Ruby growled, pushing Katie out of the way.

'Yes.'

'Why are you giving yourself a title?'

'What?'

'Why say Mrs Dodd, and not just your first name?' Ruby stepped closer, her finger outstretched towards Dorothy's face. 'Do you think you're better than us? Is that what this is all about?'

'I'm Arthur,' her husband quickly interjected, stepping forward to try and ease the tension. 'This is my wife Ruby and my daughter Katie.'

Katie moved in to shake Dorothy's hand but Ruby pulled her away.

'The last owner of that house was murdered, in his bedroom,' Ruby spat, pointing to Timothy's old abode. 'I hope you enjoy living there as much as he did.' She stormed off.

Colin ambled out of the lorry and wobbled towards the gathering.

'Arthur,' he told Colin.

'Colin,' he told Arthur.

'You fish?' Arthur asked his new neighbour, spotting a fishing rod in the back of the lorry.

'That I do my friend,' Colin responded, putting his arm around Arthur's shoulder, 'that I do.' The two went off chatting as Martha now took her turn to introduce herself.

'I'm Martha, this is my brother Oliver.'

He walked off, taking out and lighting a cigarette, looking back at Katie's bum.

It wasn't long before Katie and Arthur were back in their kitchen, met by a furious Ruby. Trying to sneak past as she scrubbed hard at a plate at the sink, Arthur was forced to clear his throat and alerted madam to their presence. She paused for a second, she too clearing her throat, before scrubbing once more at the same plate.

'You'll rub the pattern off that,' Arthur joked.

Ruby spun around, dishcloth in hand, and yelled: 'I'll rub the bastard pattern off your face in a minute.'

It was at this precise moment that Peter entered the kitchen from outside, strolling past as he whistled.

'What's up with you?' Arthur asked his angry wife.

'Mrs Dodd! Giving herself a title. How dare she.'

'You give yourself a title all the time. You announced yourself as Mrs Edwards over the phone just this morning.'

'Shut your gob or you'll be eating this dishcloth,' she continued. Arthur sat down at the kitchen table, chuckling, as Katie sensibly dashed out of the room. 'Listen here you,' she stepped closer, dishcloth clutched as though it was a dagger, 'if you think you're getting all pally with that twat husband of hers then you've got another thing coming.'

'Hey?!'

'We're having nothing to do with them, you hear me?' She stared intently at him. 'That goes for you too, Katie,' she shouted.

'Whatever,' Katie shouted back from the living room.

'I mean it. How dare she introduce herself as Mrs Dodd.'

'Why not? That's her name.'

'You don't gain my respect by giving yourself a title.'

'A bit petty, isn't it?'

'You put weed killer on Curly's crops down at the allotment last year to stop him winning best cabbage at the horticultural show, and you call me petty?'

'That was different,' Arthur grunted back, despondent.

'Oh was it?'

'Yes.'

'How?'

'Look, the woman meant no harm in calling herself Mrs Dodd. What's all this really about?'

'You, talking about feelings?' Ruby laughed, shocked. 'You had a stroke or something?'

Arthur leant in, putting his hand on hers. 'Is it the menopause?'

She pushed his hand away and dropped the dishcloth on his face. 'No it damn well isn't. Why do men always talk down to women?'

'Well according to you, women also talk down to women,' Arthur laughed, folding his arms.

'People think they're better than us, Arthur. You and me, we've been walked on our whole lives, and I've had enough of it. They can all go to blazes, the whole crapping lot of them.' She turned to face the window above the sink, her heart pounding as she refused to let her eyes moisten.

Arthur got up and placed the dishcloth on the draining board. Ruby slowly picked it up and started scrubbing at the plate yet again.

'How about cooking some food to go on that plate?' he joked.

She grabbed the bowl out of the sink and poured the hot soapy water over his head.

Myrtleville Police Station, even on a lovely sunny morning like today, was dark and dreary inside. Perhaps this was why Neville, forever a constant fixture of the place, was standing on a chair cleaning the inside of a window. He paused, pushing his face against the wall and looking sideways at the glass with one eye shut. A smear caught his attention, and he went about removing it with the cloth. His work, however, was all in vain. Not even meticulous cleaning of the window would permit more light to penetrate through it. However, Neville had to be kept busy somehow. A nuisance, but not a convicted criminal, he could hardly be kept locked up all the time. He had had his wish, in a way. His constant pestering and troublemaking at the station had landed him a place doing such menial tasks as wiping windows. Where he had come from, and where he would ultimately end up, were unknowns. One thing was for sure, though; Neville had read *I AM DEAD*.

Sergeant Kennedy marched past towards the exit, prompting Neville to jump down off the chair and accost him.

'Where's Noose? Get me Noose!' Neville demanded as Kennedy tried to slip past him.

Kennedy seemed to drain the blood from his face, as it went ever so pale, and he gave Neville a wide-eyed exaltation by bowing his head and smiling. Neville was not taller; far from it. If anything Neville was a rather short man. Short, but not fat, he appeared to have no discernible features. No features that could be seen, of course. Kennedy, on the other hand, was tall and could pass as appealing enough to attract the sexual attention of others. Due to the bizarre action before him, Neville now found in his line of sight the top of Kennedy's head. As if to hide the very early signs of hair loss from its centre, Neville opened out the cleaning cloth and placed it down upon Kennedy's head.

Sergeant Stephen Noble, looking rather rough and unshaven, pulled up in his car at the top of Myrtle Mews cul-de-sac. He looked across at Ruby and Arthur's house, knowing who was currently inside. Peter Smith. The two had not come face to face with each other again since Noble threatened him in the hospital, but he had had increasingly ill thoughts towards Peter. He was forever tracing his movements, ensuring he did not make contact with Lauren, and researching again and again his police file. There was much that Noble now knew about Peter. More than Peter knew about himself. Peter's amnesia had not eased. Not yet. And, Peter *HAD* made contact with Lauren since Noble had threatened him. Only once. But once was enough.

The sergeant looked down between his legs. His penis was out, standing up and looking at him. The eye almost winked and Noble felt it was trying to be funny with him. Intending at first to either strangle or pull it off, he put his palm around it and started squeezing, gradually pulling up and down. He looked at himself in the rear-view mirror and licked his lips, making kissing noises.

Inside the house, Peter was in the shower. He too had found his penis erect, and had also sought to deal with it. Almost flattened against the tiled wall as the hot water rushed on and around him, he thrashed at it as he thought of Lauren. But, disappointedly, he felt this insufficient stimulus and his penis went limp. Unable to satisfy himself, he reasoned to call it off and continued to merely wash.

Soon afterwards, Peter's nude body stepped out of the shower. Steam rising around him, he waved his hand in the mist to feel for the towel draped over the radiator. Something queer must have befallen him, for he suddenly went from feeling very refreshed to feeling light-headed and overwhelmed with the damp atmosphere. He collapsed, convulsing. The clatter brought Katie to the door, but it was locked from the inside.

'What are you doing in there?' she called out, to no reply.

Peter's head, having just missed hitting the toilet, vibrated as it filled with something or other from sometime or someplace other than here. He was sitting with his mother, waiting for his brother Stuart and his wife Diane to arrive. In the split second this bizarre image shot into the forefront of his mind, Peter knew he had not only seen this before, but lived it. And yet, it was in the future. It had, if linear time was to be believed, yet to happen.

Now Ruby banged on the door. By this time Peter had gotten to his feet and, wrapping the towel around himself, unlocked the door.

'What was the big bang?' Ruby asked him. This was the worst thing she could say, for memories of things yet to happen once again seized the clean man. A dumbbell nearly hitting him on the head, rolling down the stairs, rolling down the street. How strange, he thought, what could it all possibly mean? There was no sense to any of this. And then, the creepiest of them all; a new memory, a vision, became his new focus as he set eyes on Katie. There she was, bound and gagged and held elsewhere than her current location outside the bathroom door. What was all this? Peter, saying only that he'd slipped out of the shower, pushed past his audience and rushed up the ladder to the attic bedroom.

Kennedy rang the doorbell, looking at Noose. Both had come to the aid of damsels in distress before, but this case was a little stranger than usual. Noose, if not Kennedy, had been used to solving the sort of crimes that involved elderly ladies slaying their neighbours and long forgotten children plotting their parents' downfalls. Indeed, this case was, for Noose at least, a little tedious. It involved pussies, yes, but pussies who had been catnapped.

'Reckon there's anybody in?' Kennedy asked his superior. Noose now rang the bell, pressing harder than Kennedy had.

Suddenly the door swung open and there stood a woman in her mid-thirties. Her hair was short, her height was excessive. She giggled, coughing, swaying from side to side as if to show how her loose-fitting waistcoat could swish about at her instruction.

'Hello, I'm Detective Inspector Henry Noose, and this is my colleague Detective Sergeant-'

'Kennedy,' he interrupted, holding his hand out. The woman took his hand, but not to shake it. She turned it over and analysed the palm.

'Oh dear, oh deary me,' she exclaimed, bursting into yet more laughter.

'What? What is it?' Kennedy demanded, his gaze now focussed on his palm as well.

staring up at Ruby and Arthur's house. Noose tapped on the car roof and peered in. 'Sergeant, what in God's name do you think you're playing at? We've all been worried sick about you.'

Noble, without even acknowledging Noose's presence, started the engine up and drove off.

Having nothing else really pressing, Noose was sitting in his office studying the letter sent to Leah from the catnapper. Now sealed in a plastic wallet, he handed it to Kennedy as he entered the room and walked up to the desk.

'Have Lauren take a look at this. Fingerprints, anything.'

'Erm, pardon my asking, Inspector…'

'Yes, Sergeant? Are you going to ask why such a senior department of the police is working on the case of a bunch of stolen cats?'

'Well, it is kind of, well, you know…'

'Not as serious as murder?' Noose asked with a wry smile. Kennedy nodded hesitantly. 'Come now, let us savour the fact that no murders have occurred today.'

'Yet, Inspector. Yet.'

Kennedy, letter in hand from the catnapper, made his way towards Lauren's department. Passing him in the corridor was Neville, who gave him a knowing wink.

'I know all about everything,' Neville whispered as he passed him.

'I know you do,' Kennedy replied, not stopping.

Ruby looked out of the kitchen window as the new neighbours moved in. 'Mrs Dodd indeed,' she muttered to herself. 'We'll have to see about that, won't we?' The phone rang. 'Yes?' she yelled down it as she picked it up. 'Peter? I'll just get him for you.' She rested the phone on her shoulder and howled throughout the house, 'PETER! THE PHONE.'

'Hello?' the lodger responded, picking the upstairs phone up. 'Oh, Mrs Westbury! Blimey, sorry. Yes, I'll be there right away. Just give me five minutes… Thank you very much indeed… Yes, and you.' He came galloping down the stairs, combing his hair. 'I'm just off out for an hour,' he announced as he passed Ruby, who had been listening to the telephone conversation.

Mrs Westbury's house was just around the corner, and Peter made it there with a minute to spare from the promised five she had granted him upon his request.

'I'm terribly sorry,' Peter kept on sickly, 'I'm lost in the days of the week.'

'Oh don't worry lad, it's only grass.'

'Doesn't cut itself, though!'

He made his way to the shed to get the mower out.

Colin, too, was mowing the lawn in the back garden as Dorothy set up the barbecue.

'I want to invite all the neighbours to this, really make an impression,' she called out over the mower to her husband.

'Like you made with that Ruby woman?'

'Hah! She's not invited.'

Colin stopped mowing and focussed his attention on his wife. 'Look, shouldn't we start unpacking all the stuff before the next lorry load comes? We can have this barbecue any time.'

'Colin!' she growled. 'Who's the boss, eh?'

'Me?' he asked childishly.

'Hah! Now finish that lawn.'

He sighed, but did as he had been told.

Meanwhile, mere feet away, Arthur walked into the bedroom he shared with his loving wife only to clap eyes on her spying out of the window.

'Oh come on, give it a rest,' he told her. She pushed past him and jogged down the stairs, straight to the kitchen window. Arthur followed, blocked for some of the way by a slouching Katie, who dropped in a chair at the kitchen table and sighed. 'What's up with you, happy face?' he asked his daughter.

'I need a job.'

'No, you want a job. There's a crucial difference between desire and necessity. Sponging off the state is also a viable option.'

'Is this 'cause all your friends have one?' Ruby butted in, speaking down to Katie in a little baby voice.

'Well, sort of. But I need some extra money anyway.'

'Well why don't you go and ask Alex if there are any jobs going in *LENNON'S*?'

'Been there, done that.'

'Well I'm sure Tarrant would give you a job. He always employs teenage girls.'

'Hmm.'

'Go on, naff off,' she demanded of the skulking teen. Katie did just that, and now Ruby's attentions turned to her loitering husband. 'And what about you?'

'What about me?'

'When are you gonna start sorting yourself out on the job front?'

'Desire and necessity, Ruby, desire and neces-'

'Don't give me that clap trap. I work my finger to the bone for you lot, and what do I get in return? Shown up in front of our new neighbours, that's what.'

'Oh for crying out loud, you showed your bloody self up.'

All that could be said of Ruby's response was that a loud noise was involved.

'Hey Emma, are there any jobs going here?' Katie called out to her friend, who was busy replenishing a shelf with tinned cat food.

'Hey Katie. No, I doubt it. Not getting enough customers to warrant it. All that seems to be selling is cat food. What about asking Gerty?'

'Why, what could she do?'

'She's got loads of contacts. Remember all that business with Michelle's dad? Plus she's always looking for exploitable youths, isn't she.'

'Hmm. Well, it's worth a try I suppose. Thanks Emma!'

As Katie left the shop, Craig entered. That his name *WAS* Craig was known to everybody. He was the village idiot. Not in a nice, charming way. He was designated the role due to his unfortunate mentality. Nobody had ever managed to put their finger on what exactly was different about him, but there definitely was something different. This difference was seized upon as a reason to single out and isolate him. He was perhaps in his forties, and his parents were now dead. Living alone, he had clearly found it difficult to look after himself. A dirty old raincoat hung from his increasingly thin body, and a pair of spectacles he had not had changed since he was a teenager sat on his face. There were also several cuts to his face, likely made from shaving attempts. Emma was not one to go against the grain and embrace him, in fact she dodged behind an aisle precisely to avoid him. He did have this peculiar smell - a smell that lingered in the nostrils of the sniffer long after it had dispersed into the stratosphere.

Craig reached the counter as Tarrant appeared from the back room. He fumbled nervously to get his wallet out of his raincoat pocket, knowing Tarrant's glare was fixed down on him.

'Is it even raining outside?' Tarrant sneered.

'Pardon?' Craig asked, dropping his wallet. His mouth drooped somewhat on the side, even when he was talking, and a tiny drop of dribble now fell from it onto the counter as he stood upright with his wallet in-hand.

'People don't generally wear raincoats when it's not raining,' Tarrant continued his bullying.

'I've, I've,' Craig fumbled once more, the dribble now increasing in volume. He punched at the side of his leg with his free hand as he struggled to speak his words more clearly.

'WHAT - DO - YOU - WANT?' Tarrant shouted slowly. 'MORE - CAT - FOOD? You keep clearing us out of the damn stuff. How many cats do you even have?' Craig suddenly looked agog, his entire frame bouncing up and down even though his feet remained fixed. 'Oh for the love of God.'

'I've, I've won big,' Craig stuttered, brandishing a scratch card from his wallet and flashing it in front of Tarrant's shocked, squinting eyes.

'Fucking hell.' He sat down on a stool beside the till, taking a hanky from his shirt pocket and mopping his brow. He struggled to his feet, looking again at the amount. 'Big? That's bigger than my big fat stomach.' His breathing deepened as though he was having a panic attack. Or worse. 'I could have lipo with that. Balls, women wouldn't care a toss if I was fat or thin with all that,' he mumbled to himself. He looked back at Craig. Innocent, unknowing Craig. 'Look, let me just take hold of it for a second.' But Craig would not, pushing it back into his wallet and ramming it deep into his pocket once more. 'Okay, listen. You've come to the right place. I know about these things. I don't keep that sort of money on the property you see.'

'I'm not sure what you have to do, to, to claim it,' Craig explained.

'No, of course not, but I do. What you do is… I have to get a form, see, get this form sent to me by courier, yes. A form which we both then have to fill in, and send the scratch card off. You then get, erm, sent a cheque in the post for the money.'

'Oh I see. Well, if you do that and I'll come back tomorrow?'

'I could always keep the card here in my safe for, well, safe keeping?' Tarrant offered, overcome with joy at his scheming.

'I'll come back tomorrow.'

'You do that. The courier will be sure to have come.' Tarrant grimaced as Craig turned to leave, catching hold of his arm. 'Be sure not to shout this about, or go anywhere else.'

'Thank you, thank you very much.'

Craig left and Emma, now kneeling on the floor and having heard the whole thing, peeped out from behind a stack of tampons to catch the sight of Tarrant rubbing his sweaty hands together.

'Yes, see you tomorrow,' he whispered under his breath, laughing, as he disappeared behind the curtain into the back room.

TWO

Gerty, having walked from the wheelchair in the hallway to her living room armchair with ease, now flicked through the channels on the TV. She yawned, but not from lack of excitement, as the doorbell rang.

'Come in, come in, whoever you are,' she called out joyously. The door slowly opened and Katie gingerly crept in. 'Oh, it's you,' Gerty responded in disappointment when Katie made herself known.

'What are you watching?' Katie asked, glancing at the device which currently held Gerty's attention.

'None of your beeswax.' She turned the TV off. 'What do you want?'

'I'm looking for a job, Mrs Hinklebottom.'

'Are you now? You're out of luck! That crook Peter sorts my garden out. Keeps my bush neatly trimmed, he does.'

'Why do you hire somebody who nearly got you put in prison?' Katie asked, sitting on the sofa.

'He's cheap… And did I say you could sit down?'

'Erm.' She stayed seated. 'Surely you know someone who would give me a job?'

'Well I'm sure I could find one or two men who could think of a job you could do for them.' Gerty smirked, narrowing her eyes.

'Gardening?'

'Oh, I don't know about that. There may be bushes involved.'

'Look, I'll do anything.'

Gerty leant forward. 'The spider has finely caught the fly.'

'Hey?'

'You'd do anything, would you?'

'Within reason. I'm not touching your feet or anything creepy like that.'

'My dear little freckled friend, the diabetes has seen off all the discernible features of my feet yonks ago.'

'I'm sorry to hear that,' Katie replied in earnest, indeed troubled by Gerty's apparent plight.

'If you're serious, I might be able to seek employment on your behalf.'

'Doing what?'

'Something top secret.' She winked. 'Dastardly!'

'Undercover?'

'Oh no. Outdoors, in all weather.'

Katie's shoulders sank. 'Not a flippin' paper round?'

'A paper round!'

'How exactly is that top secret?'

'Well, you'll not only be delivering the paper but also some leaflets I'm having printed. The leaflets are just between you and I, of course. The newspaper people needn't be troubled with the knowledge of its distribution alongside their silly rag.' She picked her phone up and dialled a number. 'Hello, Myrtle Herald?' she shouted down it. 'Yes, Gertrude Hinklebottom here. She'll take the job,' she rolled, slamming the phone down as quickly as she'd picked it up.

'Have you planned this already?'

'Such accusations!' Gerty chuckled as Katie flopped against the back of the sofa in tumultuous teenage tiredness.

Peter, carrying a bin bag full of grass in each hand, made his way down Mrs Westbury's garden path. She waved him off, her floppy fingers flailing from side to side as the rest of her hand moved back and forth.

He headed back to Myrtle Mews, which was really just around the corner, and upon arrival spotted Ruby and Arthur's garden waste bin on the pavement outside their house. Opening the lid, he emptied the grass clippings into it.

'Hello there!' a voice called out as Peter merrily went about his business. He looked around, catching sight of Colin's head appearing above the garden fence. 'I'm Colin. You must be Arthur's son.'

'Hi. Oh, no, no, nothing like that. I'm Peter. Peter Smith.'

'Oh, I see. THE Peter Smith?'

'What do you mean?'

'I've heard all about you.' Colin smiled, winking. Peter couldn't understand. Perhaps Arthur had told him something. 'Erm,' Colin continued, are you lot up for a barbecue this evening?'

'I suspect so.'

'Good. See you about six.'

'Well, I've got a few things to do I'm afraid, but I'll send the others across definitely.'

'Righteo, please yourself!' Colin winked again, his head vanishing down behind the fence once more.

Ruby, flames almost bursting from her fierce face, tore the back door open and growled at Peter: 'Were you just talking to THEM?' All Peter could do was grin. Luckily she had not seen him dump the grass in the bin, otherwise he may have been in trouble for doing that too.

In the living room, Peter managed to convey to Arthur, via partly miming and partly whispering very, very quietly, that the barbecue was at 6pm. Arthur nodded contentedly from his sprawled position on the sofa. Meanwhile, Katie came in and flopped down in the armchair.

'Well, I've got a job,' she announced proudly, folding her arms. Ruby marched in, pleased as a dog with two.

'Good, you can start paying me keep now.'

'What?' Katie shot back, astonished.

'50% of your gross income should suffice, for now. And I'm being lenient there.'

'But… I'll barely be earning anything as it is. It's a paper round, I'll have nothing left!'

'Not my problem, Katie, you should have thought about that before getting a job. Oh, and you'll use that old pram out of the garage. I'm not having you getting a bad back carrying a load of papers.'

'No wonder dad doesn't work,' Katie cried back. 'This is so unfair, it's cruel.'

'How dare you answer me back,' Ruby shouted at her.

'How dare you even have sex with *HIM*,' she pointed at Arthur, who looked shocked and hurt, 'and create me in the first place. This is all your fault.' She stormed out, bashing her feet on each of the thirteen steps leading upstairs to her bedroom, where she presently slammed the door shut.

Ruby dropped into the armchair herself, sighing. 'Terrible, innit. Our own daughter yelling like a mongrel. I dunno where she gets it from, you know, I really don't.' At this, Arthur raised an eyebrow. She looked up at Peter, narrowing her eyes. 'You know what, she's only started acting like this since *YOU* came here.'

'Eh?' Peter blurted back, straightening his back.

'Yeah, that's right, you know,' Ruby continued, her eyes darting about as she rubbed her cheek and recalled in her mind what she believed were memories. 'Ever since we took you in, things have been happening around here. Odd things. Murders and the like. It's like we're all going mad.'

'Well *YOU* are, you daft mare,' Arthur chuckled at his wife. Ruby, lost in her own thoughts, hadn't heard her husband and thus hadn't jumped up to clack him in response.

'Listen, I'm not to blame for all this. It's like Arthur said, you're going through the menopause,' Peter responded hastily. 'And Katie's probably on her period or something.'

'What's the menopause got to do with this?' she demanded, standing.

'Well, you haven't been altogether calm and collected since I came here. You've sort of, well, started going a bit crackers as well. Maybe it's just coincidence, in conjunction with the change.'

'I'm bloody sick of this.'

'Sick of what?'

'I'm not even 50 yet. I could still bear a child if I wished. I'm nowhere near the menopause, and I'm absolutely fed up to the back teeth of you two fools going on about it. Get out, why don't you,' she squealed, leaping up.

'You what?' Arthur snorted.

'Go on, the pair of you, why don't you both sod off and don't come back.'

She grabbed them both by the scruff of the neck so quickly and tossed them out into the kitchen and through the backdoor that they couldn't resist.

Noose strolled into the police station forensic lab and yawned. There stood Lauren at a desk, a computer blazing in front of her. The brightness caught the fairness of her hair, even though it was so tightly pulled back in a ponytail as to likely cause considerable strain on the face below. Indeed, Lauren did not seem to smile as Noose approached her, which was peculiar. Usually she was beaming with joy at catching sight of her favourite father figure. Perhaps her mind was elsewhere.

'Any luck?' Noose asked her. Her smooth, pointed face remained fixed on the computer screen.

'We've got a match on a fingerprint taken off the letters. Looks like our assailant was done for shoplifting cat food in a pet shop a while back.'

'Kidnapping cats though?' Noose mused. 'That's pretty much up there in the peculiar crimes category.'

Now she turned to him. 'Is this really how our money is being spent? Tracking down a catnapper?'

Noose chuckled. Lauren raised an eyebrow - even more than it was already raised by the pull of her scalp.

'Look, I'll go round to this person's house first thing tomorrow morning. Don't want to be seen to be putting all our resources into this case, do we?'

'Precisely my sentiments, Inspector,' she agreed, emotionless. Noose turned to leave, but suddenly spun around to face her once more.

'Oh yes, I spotted Stephen.' He paused, studying Lauren's reaction. There WAS no reaction. 'Lauren?'

'Where?'

'Hanging around Myrtle Mews... where Peter is staying. He wouldn't do anything stupid, would he?'

'You know him as well as I do.'

'Well, anyway, he'll be suspended indefinitely unless he reports into the station in the next 24 hours.'

'I'll be sure to tell him, if I see him.' She looked up and forced a strange smile. Noose backed away, exiting.

The barbecue was in full swing in Dorothy and Colin's back garden. Surf songs played in the background as Colin and Arthur swigged at their cans of lager. Dorothy busied herself at the barbecue, intermittently pricking sausages and flipping burgers. Katie, Emma, Alex and Martha were all sitting around a plastic garden table, chatting away. In fact, Martha hadn't taken her eyes off Alex the whole time. He, dating Katie but with roving eyes for every other girl who caught his line of sight, had been checking Martha out. She was, perhaps, not quite his type. However, he and Katie had been going out some time now and nothing had yet occurred. He was a lad, when all was said and done. He may have been a bit wet behind the ears, but he knew sex was enjoyable. Well, from what he'd downloaded off the internet, he "knew" sex was enjoyable. Katie was a little shy, of course, and a little nervous. The two had held hands and kissed. That was about it. Thus, this Martha was a veritable feast for his moistened appetite as he sat daydreaming of great wonders in the back garden. It had not escaped Katie's attention, and she presently poked and prodded him for eye contact. He relented, being a weak sort of lad, but managed to slip in a cheeky glance in Martha's direction every time she opened her mouth. What a mouth, Alex thought.

'Going well, don't you think?' Dorothy called out to Colin, who raised his can in the air and grinned. 'Dunno why I'm doing the damn cooking. Isn't barbecuing a man's job?'

'You've got her well-trained,' Arthur laughed to Colin.

'Aye, maybe you need to train your wife a bit better,' Dorothy scolded him back. But, he found it ever so funny and rolled about with laughter.

'We're icons, you and me Colin, icons of a bygone era,' Arthur continued. Colin picked up the remains of a burger off his plate and saluted Arthur with it.

Meanwhile, Ruby spied on the whole affair from the relative comfort (and recent non-activity) of her bedroom.

'They'll pay for this, the traitors,' she mumbled under her breath. Peter, having heard her, walked in.

'You're going a bit over the top about all this, aren't you Ruby?'

'Well you haven't joined them have you, so you must side with me.'

'I'm just anti-social.' He walked out.

Back in the garden, Martha plugged her ears with her fingers as a particularly cringe-worthy song started blaring out of the speakers. Colin and Arthur began singing along. 'Shall we go in to listen to some decent music?' she asked her new friends.

'Yeah, we're up for that,' Emma replied.

'Hmm,' Katie pondered, pulling Alex aside as Emma and Martha walked towards the house. 'I'm not so sure we should go in there. Who are these people anyway?'

'Oh Katie, what are you on about now?'

'We dunno what they have planned. That house is cursed, it's always attracted weirdos. They could be luring us into the cellar to torture us.'

'Don't be daft, these houses don't have cellars,' Alex laughed.

'What if they're planning on digging one?' Katie panicked, unreasonable.

'Then we'll keep an eye out for a skip full of soil.' He marched on, leaving Katie on her own to decide whether or not she wished to join him and the others. She thought for a second, dashing after him towards the patio doors into the house.

Inside they found Oliver, sitting on a plastic storage box watching a crudely set-up TV.

'What have you brought these losers in here for?' he grumbled, slouching forward.

'Just ignore him,' Martha reassured Emma, Katie and Alex, 'he's just going through his young man desperate for sex but can't get any stage.'

'Hah, and like any of you lot have ever had sex,' Oliver responded. He looked at Katie and Alex, who were holding hands. 'I mean, look at Mr and Mrs Perfect there. Holding hands? Dumbasses. Had sex? Doubt my arse they have. Losers.' Alex, his face swelling like a beetroot, dropped Katie's hand. 'See that look in his eye?' Oliver continued, standing. 'That's the look of a virgin.'

'Think I'll head off now,' Alex told the others, turning to leave.

'Well I'm staying,' Emma responded, twirling her hair as she gazed at Oliver. He looked past her and at Katie.

'Yeah, come on Alex,' Katie chipped in.

'You gonna run, pussy?' Oliver kept on at him, stepping closer. Alex, though nervous, squared up to his aggressor and retained eye contact just long enough to ease Oliver's glare into a grin. 'Take a seat, dude. Chill.' He stepped aside, indicating for Alex to sit in front of the TV where he had just been. Alex did so, clearly now giving Oliver the advantage. Both lads felt the same; Oliver was the more dominant. It was a battle, fought out in almost utter silence and non-contact.

'I'll get some more drinks,' Martha cut in, trying to ease the tension with a bit of a skip and a giggle as she darted into the kitchen. Oliver, not sitting down with the others, stared at Katie. Alex stared at Oliver.

'Okay, bored already. Must we all stare at each other?' Emma asked.

'Nobody's staring at you,' Katie sighed.

'Oh, thanks.'

'You need constant entertainment,' Oliver snapped at Emma, 'a symptom of our society.'

Katie stood up. 'I'm just gonna pop home to the loo.'

Martha popped her head around the door. 'Go here.'

'Erm, okay.'

Katie gingerly made her way out of the room and up the stairs.

'I'm outta here,' Oliver grunted, following Katie up the stairs. Alex pondered the situation with suspicion, rubbing his chin.

Meanwhile outside, Ruby grabbed hold of the garden waste bin to move it off the pavement. She froze, horror and excitement flushing through her body as she felt the weight of it. Having just been emptied, it should not have been this heavy. She carefully opened the lid and peered inside. There, at the bottom, were the grass clippings Peter had dumped earlier. Her eyes widened with both anger and joy.

'What's up?' Peter asked, appearing at the back door.

'Grass clippings,' she seethed.

'Ah yes, I meant to tell you about them.'

'It's them isn't it, I saw that Colin and *MRS DODD* cutting their grass earlier.' She looked across at her own, uncut grass. 'Use my bin? Haha, we'll see about that.' She stormed off around the side of the house.

'No, you've got it all wrong,' Peter whimpered, almost half-wanting whatever Ruby was going to do to happen.

Upstairs in the Dodd household, Katie flushed the toilet. She washed her hands rather meticulously, before opening the door to leave. Suddenly Oliver appeared from within the bedroom where Timothy had been murdered some time prior.

'This is my room. It's the room that man was murdered in, isn't it?'

'That's right,' Katie replied, feeling very cold all of a sudden. But, she did not want Oliver to warm her up. He stepped forward and grabbed hold of her hand.

'So you like holding hands, do you?' He pulled her into his bedroom and slammed the door shut, pushing her up against it. 'You're a fine girl. Why are you with that idiot?' He tried to kiss her, but she kneed him in the bollocks and ran out of the room as he dropped to his knees in total agony, his eyes bulging as his scrotum swelled.

Katie galloped down the stairs, ready to shout out about Oliver. However, she was overruled by a much louder, more established voice, howling outside. It was her mother; and Martha, Emma and Alex had all stepped back into the garden to see what all the commotion was about. Katie joined them.

'Use my bin for your grubby grass cuttings, will you?' Ruby yelled over the fence as Arthur smirked, hiding much of his face with the can of lager.

'We don't know what you're talking about,' Colin groaned, maybe starting to regret having ever come here to Myrtle Mews.

'Let me handle this, Colin,' Dorothy took over, stepping forward.

'Ooo, bossy cow aren't ya… *MRS DODD*,' Ruby spat back.

'Why don't you just sod off, alright? You've caused us nothing but grief so far,' was Dorothy's defiant, and truthful, response. Ruby disappeared. 'That told her.' She turned to the gathering and grinned, feeling a victory was now under her belt. Sadly it was not to be, as Ruby quickly appeared once more, this time holding a hosepipe. She spun the nozzle around, turning the jet to high-pressure, and hosed Dorothy down. The whole gathering simultaneously wept in astonishment as Ruby proceeded to spray them all, including an extended stay over the barbecue; rendering it and the food absolutely useless. Arthur, too, got a violent shower, and dived for cover by tipping the table over and hiding behind it. Dorothy, frozen to the spot in shock, shook with the cold as her hair clung to her face.

Peter poked his head over the fence next to Ruby to survey the unfolding carnage - carnage he had partly caused. He couldn't help but find it funny, and dipped back down behind the fence to make sure nobody saw the big smile on his face.

It was the middle of the night, and Dorothy and Colin's back garden was still strewn with the remnants of the bombed barbecue. Vacated chairs lay in all manner of positions around the sad space, and upturned tables the only real evidence that men (or, more precisely, Arthur) had once fought for their dryness here. It was all in vain - Ruby's determination to drench them had won through. One of the patio doors slid open, and Oliver stepped out, a hood covering most of his features. He looked around at the garden, not really interested in it. He had other things to do, and headed out into the street to do them.

Also out was Peter, for some strange reason. He had not slept soundly at night for some time, yes, but he had usually remained indoors and merely tossed and turned all night. He was deep in thought, wondering whether he was remembering things about his past or simply making things up in his mind to fill in the void left by his memory loss. Nevertheless, he heard a noise up ahead as he entered Myrtle Mews, and quickly crept behind a car. Oliver jogged past, his hands thrust into his pockets.

Oliver looked around, before slipping over the fence into the back garden. However, this was not his own house. This was where Craig lived, and what Oliver was up to was anybody's guess. Luckily he had not looked around enough, and thus had missed the fact that Peter had followed him here. Intending to halt whatever was about to occur, Peter now attempted to ascend the fence. As he peeped over, he caught sight of Oliver taking out a crowbar from inside his jacket and starting to force Craig's back door open. Peter's desire to fight crime took hold, and he felt sure he would be rewarded well for foiling burglary. Suddenly, however, a hand appeared from the darkness and wrapped itself over Peter's mouth. Struggling to get free, Peter fought with his attacker but was knocked out cold with a single blow to the head and dragged into the deep darkness of this pleasant little village.

Craig was busy sitting on the toilet, his pyjama bottoms around his ankles. Joyously he went about his business, glancing around the bathroom he knew so well. After all, he had lived in this house his whole life. His parents had left it to him, along with a healthy stash in the bank. It was kept in trust, of course, invested well enough to likely see Craig out but dished out regularly enough so as not to see him short. However, what filled the man at this silly late hour was the scratch card he'd won big on. He felt sure he'd have all this in one go, and could do as he pleased with it. He was not a foolish man. In fact, he saw himself as the only truly sensible one around. He was aware how everybody else viewed him. This did hurt, but not significantly. He had been spared the desire for sex, most importantly, and felt he had been given an easy life because of it. He felt sure he would never have been able to secure a partner, had he wished for one, because of his stuttering and dribbling. He didn't have to, and this was marvellous. All he needed were cats. Lots and lots of cats. Other people's cats, even. Now that vast wealth was just around the corner for him, he had visions of moving away to a cottage somewhere in the countryside with acres and acres of land. He could be far away from other humans, and really close to hundreds of cats. He would start a cat sanctuary, taking in strays (and also simply taking, without the permission of the owners).

Just now, he stood up and wiped his bottom. But there was something not right, in the bath. A shower curtain was fixed over the bath as Craig's mother had had an electric shower fitted on the wall above the bath just before she died. She was always afraid Craig would fall asleep in the bath and drown. But, couldn't he also slip on the soap if he was stood up in the bath and bang his head? Neither of these accidents were to end his life. No, because Craig looked over at the shower curtain pulled across the bath and felt something wasn't right. Pyjama bottoms still around his ankles, Craig edged forward to investigate, pulling the curtain open. There, in the bath, stood a looming figure in a cat mask. Craig's mouth dried for the first time he could remember, and he made for the door as the figure brandished a gigantic knife.

Although it had been second nature finding his way around this house in the dark, Craig now lost all notion of location and tumbled down the stairs. The figure in the cat mask slowly followed as Craig came crashing to the bottom. He dropped against the front door, his head pressed against the letterbox.

'Meow!' the figure exclaimed, purring as they thrust the knife down into Craig's head and left it there. The village idiot wept as he died, his last image on this earth, before his blood sealed his eyelids shut, being his killer doing a dance at the bottom of the stairs whilst they licked the back of their hand and rubbed their head with it.

THREE

It was, yet again, a glorious day to be alive. The sun blazed, the birds tweeted, cats roamed freely. Well, some of them. Katie, however, was not glad to be alive. Pushing a rusty old pram full of newspapers, she arrived outside Craig's house and made her way down the drive to post the paper. When she tried to do so, she found it somewhat of a struggle. There seemed to be something blocking the letterbox, something resting against it from the inside. Of course, Craig's corpse lay against it, the knife sticking out of his head. His head jerked forward as Katie persisted with the paper from outside, eventually winning the battle when Craig's body flopped sideways and the paper opened out and landed on his face. As Katie strolled back to the pram on the pavement, Noose pulled up in his car. Yawning, he stepped out and waved to Katie as she carried on down the road. He walked up to Craig's front door and banged on it loudly. Nobody answered, and Noose bent down and opened the letterbox to look through. Nothing was visible, so he walked to the side of the house and into the back garden.

At the back was the evidence of forced entry Peter had been about to witness. The back door was ajar, the lock had been forced, but Noose also noticed a window was broken further along. Fearless, he pushed the door open and stepped inside. Greeted first by the smell, and then the sight, of a plethora of cats roaming freely around the house, Noose petted one of them as it rubbed against his legs. Then he walked into the hallway and found Craig's corpse. He looked on, annoyed. 'Brilliant!'

Sergeant Stephen Noble had moved back in with his parents George and Myra. Never fully able to escape them, he had for a time, at least, managed to dodge their grasps. However, he had not been right since he had begun to obsess more and more about Peter. Something inside him had snapped, and he kept having the overriding urge to kill Peter. Now was his chance, as he stood over the unconscious body of the man. Tied to a chair in Noble's garage, Peter's limp frame was right there and ready for slaughtering. Noble, unwashed and unshaven, paced up and down. Suddenly he stopped, dropped his trousers and got his penis out. He held it in his hands, surveying it nervously. If he could only bend down and bite it off, he would have done so. But, his ribs were in the way. Consequently, he turned and pissed into a bucket. He pulled his trousers back up and put his penis away, trying desperately to quash these recent desires to do away with it. He picked the bucket up and threw the urine over Peter's face. The shock awakened him with a start, and he looked across at Noble. Shaking the warm wet hair off his face, he looked around the garage. Empty paint tins, an old lawn mower, and a chest freezer were all that it really housed. Oh, and the two men. But, Peter didn't really feel there at all. He felt strangely uninterested, as though this would all sort itself out.

'Oh come on,' he said to Noble, who punched him square in the face.

'You should leave him you know. You can't continue to be treated that way,' Noble responded.

'What?'

Noble grabbed hold of Peter's urine-soaked hair and twisted his face towards his own. 'That's what you told Lauren to do.'

'She told you that?'

'I was listening.'

'You're a spy now, are you?'

Noble let go and wiped his hand on Peter's jumper. 'I'm glad I've got you around, Peter. You give everything an extra edge somehow.'

'Ah yes, I remember her saying that.'

'And what exactly did she mean by that?'

'Well she kissed me,' Peter grinned, 'so you tell me, Sergeant no balls.'

Noble grabbed hold of Peter's balls and squeezed as hard as he could. Peter screeched in agony. 'Glad you're around? Not for much longer. I told you to stay away from her, didn't I?' Suddenly Noble stood up straight, squeezing his mouth to the side and calling out in a high-pitched voice: 'Stephen, is that you in there?' Noble looked towards the garage door. 'Oh no, it's my mother.'

'Eh?' Peter replied, confused.

'Shut up,' Noble growled, slapping Peter across the face. 'You haven't had your breakfast yet, Stephen,' he said, again in the voice - an impression of his mother's. 'Come on out of there.' He stepped over to the chest freezer and opened the lid, pressing a finger to his lips as he peered inside. 'Shush mother, can't you see I'm busy?' he whispered into the freezer, lifting out a clear plastic bag with Myra Noble's head in it. He turned the bag to face Peter, like he was showing his mother what was happening. Peter shrieked in terror, screaming out for help. Noble just laughed. 'Shout all you like, nobody will hear you in here. I've prepared for this. This entire garage is sound-proofed. Nobody's coming to rescue you.'

'The meowgerie,' Kennedy chuckled, looking around a bedroom in Craig's house which was full of scratching boards and litter trays. Noose, meanwhile, cradled a cat and made kissing noises at it as dozens of others roamed about. 'I never knew you were so soft in the head, *SIR*,' was

Kennedy's amused response. Noose looked up, annoyed. 'Meowgerie - like menagerie, only for cats,' Kennedy explained his ignored joke. Noose frowned, putting the cuddled pussy down.

At the bottom of the stairs, Lauren was standing over Craig's corpse. 'Looks like one of the catnapping victims tracked him down and got angry,' she called up the stairs as Noose descended them.

'Looks that way, doesn't it. Myrtle Mews is only two streets away, no doubt Peter will be able to shed some light on all of this,' Noose remarked. Lauren did not respond, continuing with her work. 'He seems to be involved with everything these days.'

Kennedy now came down the stairs and joined Noose over Lauren. 'Big penis,' he pointed out, studying Craig's corpse.

'Hmm,' Noose replied as Lauren looked away uneasily. 'Look, you do the usual routine, Sergeant. I want to know if the neighbours heard or saw anything, and what kind of bloke this man was. Alright?'

Kennedy nodded. 'Sir.'

Ruby opened the door to Noose, who was standing impatiently on the step.

'I see, called the cops in the end did she? Wonder she didn't do it last night,' Ruby spat.

'Who called the cops?'

'Yes, I did it Inspector, but with good reason. Persecution drove me to it, persecution of the working woman. Hard-working too, don't forget that when you're making an example of me in court.'

'There has been a murder, Mrs Edwards.'

'You must be joking? I didn't kill her.'

'Not she, he.'

'Colin? That'll be Dorothy won't it… *MRS DODD*, trying

to frame me. Well I won't have it.' She slammed the door shut on Noose. He thrashed at it once more. 'I haven't murdered anyone, Inspector,' she went on as she pulled the door open again.

'I never said you had,' Noose sighed, 'please, I just came to see Peter.'

'I see, involved in it is he? I should have known. Had my suspicions about him, I have.'

'Is he in or not?' Noose shouted, getting sick of the loose canon before him.

'Nope. Ain't seen him,' Ruby responded nonchalantly. 'And there's no need to shout, either.'

Arthur presently appeared by her side. 'What's going on?'

'Oh go and lie back down on the sofa will you, that's all YOU'RE good for.'

Noose checked his watch. 'When did he go out?'

'Last night. Haven't seen him since.'

'Odd. Does he make a habit of staying out?'

'No.'

'She told him to go,' Arthur butted in. 'Told him AND me to sod off and not come back.'

'Yeah, damn right I did. So why are you still here, eh?'

'God only knows,' Arthur mused.

'Anyway, she ain't called the cops yet. What trick is she playing at?' Ruby whispered to him.

'Do I really care?' He pushed past her and walked off down the drive. 'Have a good day, Inspector.'

'And where do you think you're off to?' Ruby shouted after him.

'Fishing.'

'Who hasn't called the cops yet?' Noose questioned, intrigued by Ruby's peculiar behaviour.

'Oh don't you start,' was her quick snap back.

'Do you know a Craig Thompson, two streets away?'

'Craig Thompson...' Ruby thought, tapping her chin. 'Weirdo in a raincoat? Smells of cat wee? Hmm, never liked him. He's a bit of an oddball.'

'Well, he's been murdered.'

Katie walked past in the street, pushing her pram full of papers.

'Hey, Katie, get over here,' Ruby called to her.

Katie rolled her eyes and ambled across to them. 'What do you want, MOTHER?' She looked at Noose. 'If you're here about last night, then she did it.'

'Did she indeed?'

'She soaked everyone. Humiliated me in front of the entire street, my friends and, more importantly, my boyfriend.'

'No, no, it's not about that. It's about that man who dribbles.'

'What was it, a fake one?'

'A fake what?' Noose asked.

'Go ask Emma, she told me he came into the shop yesterday with a scratch card. He'd won big apparently. Mr Tarrant tried to get it off him, then told him a pack of lies to lure him back with it today.'

'I see.'

Noose entered TARRANT'S, immediately catching sight of Gerty and Sharon.

'That one,' Gerty demanded, pointing at a bunch of bananas. Sharon picked them up and put them in the basket she was holding. 'No, no. Take them out. I only want one banana off that bunch.' Sharon lifted the bunch out and, placing the basket on the floor, pulled one of the bananas off the bunch and placed that in the basket. 'And, one off that bunch also,' Gerty carried on, pointing out another bunch. Sharon pulled one off that too. This went on until Gerty had six separate bananas, one each from a different bunch. 'There.

Now, I want half a loaf.' Sharon pushed Gerty over to the bread and took a loaf off the shelf, opening it and emptying out half the slices.

Noose stepped up to the counter, where Emma greeted him with a very formal: 'Inspector Noose.'

'Hi Emma. Look, I've just spoken to Katie. She told me that Craig Thompson came in here yesterday with a winning scratch card?'

'Yes, why?'

'Do you know how much it was for?'

'No, but I know it must have been a lot.'

'Why?'

'Well, Mr Tarrant said women wouldn't mind about his big stomach if he had that kind of cash.'

'I see.'

'Yeah,' Emma continued, 'he told him to come back today 'cause he had to get a courier to come and check the scratch card or something and give him a cheque.'

'So this Craig Thompson left with the scratch card?'

'Yeah, and then…' but she fizzled out, nervous. Noose narrowed his eyes. She leant forward, whispering, 'Mr Tarrant laughed. I think he intended to somehow keep the money himself you know, trick Craig out of it.'

'Interesting.'

'Oh, why?'

'I found Craig Thompson dead this morning. Murdered.' Noose smiled, Emma went pale and sullen. 'Could you tell me where I could find Mr Tarrant please, Emma?'

Suddenly the shop door swung open and Tarrant shuffled in. 'Best thing I ever did, giving you a key to open up,' he called out to Emma, burping as he rubbed at his sweaty face with an old brown rag. He ignored Noose, who turned to glare at him, as he wobbled behind the counter. 'Had a rough night. Jeez.' He flopped down on a stool and yawned.

Gerty and Sharon, who had been ear-wigging the whole time, now came to the counter as Noose asked: 'What were you doing last night, Mr Tarrant?'

'And who the hell are you?' Tarrant snapped, struggling to his feet to look Noose straight in the eyes.

'I'm Detective Inspector Henry Noose, investigating the murder of Craig Thompson,' Noose squared up to him. Tarrant began shaking, dropping the old rag. Unable to bend down and pick it up, he instead moped his oily brow with his creased Hawaiian shirt. 'Has that courier arrived yet?'

'Courier?'

'For Craig's scratch card?'

'Oh.' Tarrant took a deep breath. 'Shit.'

'Yes, Mr Tarrant, you certainly are in the shit.'

Gerty burst into laughter whilst Sharon gasped in surprise.

New best buddies Arthur and Colin had a lovely morning fishing down by the lake. From rowing a boat in tandem and comparing contents of their tackle boxes, to measuring up their fishing rods; it was a glorious memory in the making, unfolding before their "bromance" eyes. As Ruby tore her hair out at home, desperate for somebody to understand her misplaced and unexplainable fury, her husband frolicked playfully with the husband of the latest focus of her menace.

As Tarrant was being lead out of his shop for questioning, he suddenly turned on Noose and gave him a heavy smack across the face. Taken by surprise, and the weight of the vast man, he fell back into the convenience store, where Emma rushed to pick him up. Tarrant made a dash for it, moving quicker than he had ever done before, getting into his car and speeding off. However, he didn't go far, accelerating right at *LENNON'S* shop window just up the road.

Having just topped it up with papers for the rest of her

round, Katie dived out of the way as Tarrant mowed her pram down.

'This is my town, you bastard!' Tarrant screamed, as his car ploughed straight through the glass panelling and demolished everything inside the shop. Angry nobody had been surveying the fresh fruit in the window at the time, Tarrant sought further carnage by rolling out of his car and taking out a lighter. He grabbed at the collapsed newspaper stand, about to set some paper alight. However, his face suddenly went from being very red to very, very pale. His hands went limp, dropping against the sides of his stomach and bouncing up momentarily before he collapsed to his knees.

Noose rushed in just in time to see Tarrant drawing his last breaths. 'I didn't kill Craig,' he screeched out, gasping one last time. He fell forward, flat on his face, dead.

Noose returned to see Lauren in the lab. She was looking somewhat worse for wear, inattentive to either her mental or physical state. Noose noticed she seemed to be shaking, though he could not exactly pin the movement down. Either his eyes were vibrating, or it was her entire body. Her hair was pulled back tight which made it shine that dirty sort of shade, yes, but it was also lifeless and fraying at the bottom of the ponytail. They say your hair is one of the things to suffer when you're stressed. If that were true, she should have been bald by now. Noble had been the cause of much anxiety for her of late. He had left her uncaring, cold. She didn't even bother trying to dab any makeup over the heavy bags under her eyes to conceal them any more. She had never been a good sleeper. There was always something troubling her, even from an early age. It was like the dream world could lead to something that much more real than she wanted. The life she was living had been fine, but increasingly both events happening within the daytime setting and the night time dream world had become untenable. Noble featured in both, as did Peter. In her fractured dreams they were both themselves *AND* each other. Not only that, but they could each be two different people as well. Peter, in the real world, had only shown himself to be one person to her. He could not remember himself, of course, but he was caring and kind and above all else honest. In her eyes, anyway. Noble had started that way too, when she first got together with him. However, he had slowly declined into the person she saw him as when she slept. There, he was a psychopath. Plain and simple. He had been quickening his slip into this mentality, Lauren thought, since Peter had come on the scene. Noble had perceived she and Peter had something going on. They had not, initially. But, after Noble threatened Peter in his hospital bed, things changed. Peter hadn't stayed away from her like Noble demanded, had he?

'Anything?' Noose asked her.

'The house was broken into twice, believe it or not,' she replied.

'I see. The window and the door? Peculiar.'

'Yup. Two sets of fingerprints too. One set belongs to that Tarrant guy.'

'Do we have a match for the other?'

'Indeed we do. In fact, his address was just updated on our database recently to Myrtle Mews.'

Noose gulped. 'Surely not Peter?'

'No.' Lauren turned away. 'Oliver Dodd. He's already got a record for breaking and entering. There's nothing on Craig's body that links Tarrant there, but I suggest you pay this Oliver a visit. It may prove fruitful, Inspector.'

'Thanks Lauren.' He paused, studying her face for a second. She caught his glance, turning to face him.

'What?'

'Look, I'm sorry things haven't worked out with Stephen,' he uttered. She stayed silent, but did not turn away. 'But,

Lauren…' He stopped, thinking about what he wanted to get through to her. 'Peter… I've known him for a long time. Since he was a boy, in fact.'

'Why are you telling me this?'

'He has a lot of good traits. Great traits. But, seriously, so much has gone on. He can't remember, he says he can't remember.'

'I've read his file, I'm well aware.'

'He blocks things from his mind, he ignores these awful tragedies that occurred. It's not for me to say, really.'

'Then don't, Inspector,' Lauren commanded, now turning and walking away.

'Everything he touches turns into a disaster. And then… and then, everything is nothing.'

Lauren froze. 'Everything is nothing?'

'He forgets, blocks or whatever. Everything becomes nothing to him. Don't let yourself become nothing.'

Noose turned and left. Lauren, the taste of that enigmatic Peter Smith still on her lips, sobbed quietly.

Neville cleared his throat. Startled, Lauren wiped her face clean with the back of her hands, and looked furiously around for where he was hiding. Suddenly he appeared from behind her, almost like he had always been standing there. But that was impossible.

'Peter is marvellous.'

'GET OUT!' she yelled. He smiled. 'What do you mean?'

'You're meant for each other. It's written…' Neville giggled, 'in the stars.'

'Piss off,' she choked, the remnants of the sob still in her throat, pushing him towards the door.

'Lucy, all the others, they're nothing. They're not even worthy of his mention,' Neville continued cryptically.

'What are you on about?'

'It's all about you, Lauren, they don't even get a look-in.'

'What's all about me?'

'*I AM DEAD*! All this, happening right now, it's just fodder, fluff. There's a whole other existence that played out before it. You, Peter-'

'You?' she interrupted.

'Oh no!' he chuckled. 'I'm the biggest pile of padding there is.' He stepped closer, smelling her face. 'I'm so inconsequential that nobody even knows who I am.'

'Peter doesn't know who he is.'

Noose barged in. 'I thought I heard shouting!' He grabbed Neville by the scruff of the neck and yanked him away from Lauren.

'Oh shucks,' Neville giggled, as Noose dragged him out.

'Sorry about this, Lauren,' Noose sighed.

'No, wait-' she called back, but they were gone.

'Hello, I'm Detective Inspector Henry Noose,' he told Dorothy on her doorstep.

'Good, I'm glad they've sent one of the top men.'

'Well, I don't know about that, but-' Noose responded, flattered.

'Yeah, that Ruby was so out of order. She wants locking up for what she did.' She folded her arms and tutted as the horrific events of the hosepipe assault replayed over and over in her mind.

'No, I'm not here about that... whatever that is.'

'Oh?'

'I'm here to see Oliver Dodd, presumably your son.'

'Oh, here we go,' Dorothy seethed, 'startin' already is it?'

'What is?'

'The persecution of my boy! Happened in the last place we lived as well, everyone accusing him of stealing this and knickin' that.' Tears welled up in her eyes as she brought out a hanky. 'That Ruby, was it? Lodging a complaint? This is disgusting.'

'Mrs Dodd, we have fingerprint and DNA evidence to place your son at the scene of a murder and burglary last night.'

'Oh my God!' she cried, 'no wonder he ain't been back.'

'I beg your pardon?'

'Ain't seen him,' she went on, 'he must have done a runner.'

'I don't believe this!' Katie called out as she stepped into the kitchen from the back door. 'Hello, anyone in? That damn fatty manager from the shop just ran over the pram. It could have had a *FRIGGIN* baby in it.' She walked into the living room. Empty. 'Oh,' she added, an afterthought, 'then he drove into *LENNON'S* and dropped dead. Massive heart attack. Gerty said he was diabetic; used to sell his insulin to her or something.' Katie jogged up the stairs. 'Must be out.' Entering her bedroom, she flopped on the bed. Oliver appeared from behind the door, slamming it shut.

'Please, don't scream,' he begged.

'What the? Get out now or I *WILL* scream, *AND* smash your testicles into next week.'

'Katie, please, just let me speak,' he whimpered.

'How *DARE* you come in my house, in my bedroom!'

'I dunno what to do. The police are after me, it's just all such a horrible mess.'

'Why are the police after you? Are you a rapist or something?'

'I broke in, yes, but he was just there, oh God.' He held his mouth, trying not to vomit, as the knife went into Craig's head. Over and over again, Oliver saw it happening. The blood, the gore, the killer in the cat mask doing a dance. 'I could have stopped it from happening, or... I just don't know.'

All of a sudden the bedroom door opened and Noble stepped quietly in.

'Oh thank God, Sergeant Noble!' Katie breathed a sigh of relief as Noble stared at her.

'You,' Noble pronounced at Oliver, but keeping his eyes on Katie, 'Inspector Noose is in the street. Your time is up. Go.' Oliver, frozen to the spot, shook in terror. Noble grabbed him and tossed him out of the room.

He ran down the stairs and out of the house, where Noose caught a glimpse of him.

'Is that him?' Noose called back at Dorothy, who was still stood in her own doorway.

Meanwhile, Katie seemed somewhat perplexed as Noble peeped down on the street from her bedroom window. She frowned, gritting her teeth.

'What's going on? Are you arresting him or what?'

'He's the one they're after for the murder.'

She flopped onto the bed, gasping, 'I could have been killed.'

Noble smiled, turning to face her. 'You could have.'

'Katie Edwards has gone missing,' Noose bawled, sitting down and banging his fist on the table. Opposite him in the interview room sat Oliver and Dorothy. Next to Noose was Kennedy, who seemed to be blinking more regularly than usual. Oliver was not blinking at all. His face was doing nothing, giving nothing away. It was as though he had left his body. He was gone, and all that remained was this flimsy drooping sack for Noose to yell at.

'And what's that got to do with my son?' Dorothy shouted back at the inspector.

'You and I both saw him coming out of her house yesterday,' Noose explained. 'Tell me, Oliver, why were you in Katie's house?'

'What exactly are you holding him here for? The burglary, the murder... the abduction?' Dorothy blared. 'Maybe all three. He is, after all, an octopus. He can do them all at once, can't he!'

'We have both fingerprints and DNA placing him at the scene of Craig Thompson's murder.'

'She called him Sergeant Noble,' Oliver whispered.

'What? What did you say?' Noose shot back, leaning in to the teenager.

'I didn't know where else to go. I went to see her. A man came into her room.'

'Sergeant Noble?'

'That's what she called him.'

Noose looked back at Kennedy, who consciously tried to stop blinking whilst he was being looked at.

'How much longer are you going to hold my son here?' Dorothy demanded, standing up.

Noose stood up too, followed by Kennedy.

'We will be charging your son shortly, Mrs Dodd.'

Oliver was pushed into the cell, where Neville gave him a generous smile from the bed, as the cell door was slammed shut and locked on him.

'Oh dear, oh dear,' Neville trilled, sticking his tongue out. 'Haven't you been naughty?'

'Who are you?'

'I'm Neville, but you can call me… *NEVILLE,*' he laughed.

'I haven't killed anyone.'

'Yet.' Neville got to his feet, raising his head to the narrow barred window high up in the wall. 'I wonder,' he pondered, turning to Oliver. 'So what have you done? Tell me,' he stepped closer to the boy, 'what did you see?'

'How do you know?'

'Tell me what you saw.'

'Awful things. Murder.'

'How could you live with yourself, knowing that will be playing over and over in your mind for the rest of your life?'

Oliver stepped back against the wall, just below the barred

window. Neville sat back down on the bed, yawning. He lay down, turning his back on Oliver. When he turned back around some time later, the boy had hanged himself with his shoelaces from one of the bars over the window. Two police officers had rushed in and were in the process of cutting him down. Neville smiled at the face of the dead lad as his limp corpse dropped to the cell floor.

'I must have drifted off,' Neville sighed carelessly to the panicking officers.

FOUR

Peter cried as he watched Noble slap Katie across the face.

'You like hurting girls, don't you, Peter?' Noble called back to him, striking the defenceless girl again.

'You fucking bastard, I'll kill you,' Peter screamed at the vile man.

Katie was bound and gagged, just like Peter had seen her in his bizarre vision during the bathroom collapse a day or two prior. He now read a lot into that, hoping he could conjure up an image of himself breaking free from his binds and lashing out at Noble. Mere feet separated the two men, but the starvation and beatings he had been subjected to, not to mention the tight binds, held him back. Katie must have slipped into unconsciousness as Noble presently let her go. She dropped in a heap on the concrete floor as he stepped back to Peter.

'Kill me, eh? Like you killed your *FIANCÉE* Lucy, and all the other young women you have acquainted yourself with? What about Louis and James from the Museum Club?'

'So you're going to kill Katie?'

'No, *YOU'RE* going to kill Katie. Well, technically I will end her life, but *YOU* will take the rap. You'll actually get found guilty this time. There's method in my madness, you see.'

'You're certainly mad,' Peter lamented. For this insolence, Noble picked up a paint tin and smashed it across Peter's head. 'You're really willing to go *THIS* far for Lauren?' Peter continued through the pain.

'Lauren?' Noble laughed. 'This isn't even about her anymore.'

'It *IS* for me. I love her,' Peter declared. A tear rolled down Noble's cheek as he stepped back from Peter. 'And she loves me.' Noble's chest jerked forward, as though Peter had actually wrenched his heart out. 'That evening I spent with her was the best time of my entire life. That you overheard some of it doesn't take away from it. I'm glad you heard it.'

'How could you?' Noble moaned, crying.

'What, just because you told me not to? You think that was going to stop me? We're meant to be together, I know it.'

'Why?'

Peter went on:

I had been warned not to go anywhere near Lauren, and at first I planned to in some way honour this threat. Why, I don't know. It would probably have been in my nature to go against any threat and do the opposite of what it commanded. If I could remember my nature. But, on this occasion, I relented and went along with it. Initially. Of course, as the days went on, after the attempt on my life from Jim, I began to think more and more of Lauren. Something drew me to her, something I could not explain. She was perfection to me, even if but a glimmer at present. I wanted to get near, to possess her perfection and envelop all that she could offer. It was not a silly crush, oh no. I knew this because she did not have any of the hallmarks of what would warrant a crush in the first place. She was shapeless, slender and free from any endowments bestowed upon her for grabbing prying eyes. Perhaps this is what lured me in, the fact she may not draw the attention of others. She would be all mine. But, she was not. She was another man's. If, indeed, she could be possessed at all. No, she was no meat for fighting over. She could flit between whomever she so wished. I wished for her to flit to me, discarding this other man who claimed ownership over her and who had been ever so small as to threaten me. To threaten Peter Smith, of all people! The man who could not remember, but who had endlessly escaped from the clutches of psychopaths wishing for his demise. I had begun to feel invincible, immortal even. The man I was before I had forgotten myself could have been anyone. Perhaps all manner of things had happened. The dreams attested to that. After Jim's attempt on my life, my dreams had almost altogether fallen upon Lauren and Lauren alone. Most were pleasant, wondrous. Some were horrific. Sex was a main feature, of course, I am a young man after all. Lauren and I, in the throws of passion, seized my sleeping mind often. And, images of the future also graced me. We were married, with a daughter, living in a flat. All was so happy and right. Then, there were the bad dreams. Lauren was sprawled on our marital bed, dead and soaked in blood. What had happened? I felt sure she had done it to herself, but I wanted to blame someone else. It disturbed me so, but I knew I could convince my waking mind that this was mere nonsense. The fear of what could befall me should I actually get in contact with her, to do the forbidden, was playing on my mind and making me see these terrible things. We could be so happy, that much was clear. I knew I could not stay away, and I did not.

I went to her flat. She opened the door before I even had a chance to knock, almost like she knew I was coming. I had waited, waited for what felt like thousands of years and just milliseconds all at the same time. I stepped in, not even waiting for an invitation to do so, and she locked the door behind us. I explained my dreams, mentioned all manner of things.

'You should leave him you know. You can't continue to be treated that way,' I did say to her, yes.

'I'm glad I've got you around, Peter. You give everything an extra edge somehow,' she responded, taking my hand. We moved in and kissed on the lips. She tasted so wonderful. She had not brushed her teeth, so I could taste the real her. We held our lips together long enough for me to taste her breath as it entered me. I wanted more of her, I wanted to enter her. But, the time was not right at this moment. She was nervous, I could tell that. There was the unsettled, the stuff still left hanging that needed to be cleared up before we could progress together. Now that we had had this moment I could rest assured we WOULD progress. I was contented to leave it at that, for now.

'You've said all that sort of shit before, about Lucy,' Noble laughed in Peter's face. 'It's in your file. Lauren is no more different from her. She's just the latest of your victims. You and me, Peter, we're the same. Thing is, I can see that now. My eyes have been opened.'

'I don't remember Lucy.'

'And you won't remember Lauren, once you're done with her. You seize them, consume and destroy, then spit them out.' He spat on the floor, swinging behind Peter and pushing him and the chair over. He grabbed Peter by the hair and pushed his face into the spit. 'Come on, consume, seize the day!' he riled. Overwhelmed, Peter gave up and relaxed all the energy he had been forcing into his muscles. Noble sensed this, pulling him back up. 'Oh God, no,' he suddenly called out, clutching his head with one hand and outstretching the other towards Peter. 'I can see it all now, I can see everything.' Peter sat mute, inert. 'And everything is nothing.' He leant against the freezer, shaking his head. 'What is... The Space?' Peter did not respond. 'WHAT IS THE SPACE?' Noble screamed, spinning around and striking his hostage across the face. He could no longer respond, he was too far gone. Noble could not accept this, striking him again and again. Peter was resigned to his fate, just waiting there for the end to come. 'There is this thing in my head, it has been telling me, showing me. Now it reveals itself to me. It is time. But no, it is not The Space. The Space has closed. This is Reaping Icon.' He opened the freezer and took out a clear plastic bag. 'Reaping Icon tells me it is time. This is my chance.' He put the bag over Peter's head. 'Your time is up, I *WILL* usurp your link to The Space.' His words were crazy, incoherent. Peter's dry, chapped lips mouthed something through the bag. Noble did not want to hear it. His eyes dashed around the room, spotting a roll of duct tape. He grabbed it, wrapping lengths of it over the bag and tight around Peter's neck. As the bag constricted around his face and steamed up with the last of his breaths, Peter's mind suddenly flooded with memories of his past. But, they were fragmented and contradictory. He knew Lucy, he knew his mother and brother Stuart. He still was not whole, he realised there was something left incomplete.

Noose and a team of armed officers smashed the garage door down and stormed in, flooring Noble and tearing the bag off Peter's head. Peter, unconscious by now, merely thought he was dead and was willing to accept that. Noble broke free, charging out of the place, right into the middle of the road and the path of a speeding lorry. It minced his body under its vast tyres, slapping it around on the tarmac. He came to a halt, all torn and dying, as the lorry slammed its breaks on. A smiling figure appeared above him in his clouded vision. It was Reaping Icon.

'A simple task, Stephen. You have failed, just like Tony and Jim before you. All now rests on Darren. Woe betide that having happened,' Reaping Icon tutted. 'Woe betide.'

Noble knew he was a goner, and as he sealed his eyes shut for the last time he saw Reaping Icon's foot rushing down onto his face.

'I just don't know what I'll do if something's happened to her,' Alex went on at Emma, sitting next to her on her bed. 'She's just great. Really trusting too. I mean, us two just sat here now, on your bed, how many other girlfriends would be cool with that happening?'

'I guess,' Emma replied, placing her hand on his leg.

'Yeah, 'cause you're really fit, which she knows, so she must really trust me.' He looked down at the photo he clutched of himself and Katie smiling happily. But, were things really that happy between them? Katie's disappearance this last day had brought back all the happy memories he had of his time with her. He had pushed the not so happy times to the back of his mind. The times he tried to initiate something a little more than just kissing and holding hands, for example.

Emma's hand moved up his leg and he noticed. He couldn't help it. 'Why did you choose Katie?' she asked him outright.

'What do you mean, choose?'

'Well, there are other girls.' She wet her lips.

'I suppose so. I'm not exactly a Casanova or anything though, am I?'

'Oh, I don't know,' Emma replied, almost shyly.

'What do you mean by that?' he asked her, but refused to look up at her. He could feel his penis hardening in his trousers. It was not a good sign.

'I look at you both together, and it doesn't always feel-'

'Feel what?'

'Doesn't always feel natural.'

'Natural?'

'It feels forced, clumsy.' She removed her hand from his leg, but he took hold of it and put it back.

'I always thought... no, I knew... I knew I had no chance in hell with you. You're so stunning I just automatically went for Katie. You've never been on my radar.' Now he looked up at her, and she was moving in. They kissed. He undid her top as she undid his belt and trousers. His erect penis sprung out as he pulled at her bra. She unhooked it from the back and her breasts popped out. He had never done so before, but instinctively he went in with his mouth and sucked at her hard nipples. He straightened his back, moving from her breasts to get his breath back, knocking the photo of himself and Katie off the bed. It fell to the floor, face-down, as Emma took his penis in her hand and bent down to it. She placed her moist lips around the tip, not knowing quite what to do, but thinking this was what should happen next as they both progressed on this adventure. Sticking her tongue out, she licked it from the base to the tip, before putting the whole thing in her mouth and letting go. He pushed it in further, causing her to nearly choke. She flopped back, coughing. 'Sorry,' he fumbled, trying to get up off the bed in embarrassment. She grabbed his hand and pulled him down on top as she lay back, slipping her own trousers and knickers off.

He looked nervously down at her vagina, the dark hair trimmed neatly around it, as she opened her legs around him. She took his penis in her hand again.

'Do you have a condom?' she whispered, jacking his penis. But, the question was all in vain, as he screwed his face up and ejaculated on her stomach.

'Sorry,' he said yet again.

Deathly silence pervaded the Edwards' living room. The curtains were only half drawn, the blinds sealed altogether. Things weren't right, and Ruby didn't want any light. She wanted her daughter back, safe and well. Luckily the sofa was underneath her, for her body felt like concrete. She was collapsing in on herself, wracked with guilt and fear. She'd been crazy of late, and now she knew it. Arthur came slowly to her, sitting down and taking her hand. She would normally have snatched it back and given him a stern telling off, but this time she let him. Desperately she wanted the comfort and security of her husband.

'She'll be fine,' he told her, hoping his mind would agree with these automated words.

'Don't say a word,' she uttered back, rubbing the back of his hand and leaning in to give him a quick kiss. It was the first kiss they'd shared for a while. Things had been tough, strained, recently - ever since Peter Smith had come to stay. This is what now occupied Ruby's mind. Doing well to forget Katie's current unknown status, she filled herself with questions about Peter. Why had she just gone along with him staying? The family didn't know him from Adam, and yet had just bowed down and let him walk all over them. They had treated him as one of their own, elevating him to the top of the house in the attic. He had done whatever he pleased, getting away with it in the process. How he even first arrived at their house now seemed somewhat hazy in Ruby's mind, the details strangely out of reach. This didn't matter, though. All that mattered was that his position in the house, in their *HOME*, was now untenable. He simply had to go.

The phone rang. Arthur got up to answer it, but Ruby kept hold of his hand. She didn't want to hear it. She felt sure Katie was dead. She couldn't bear it. To lose Katie would be the end of it all for her. She and Arthur had tried and tried for a child for twelve long years, all but giving up when she fell pregnant by surprise. Why was she so hard on Katie? It was just her nature, and Katie knew that. Arthur prized his hand away and picked the phone up. It was Noose, phoning ahead, with good news of course. Katie had been found, alive, and not too badly hurt. Bruises would heal. The mental damage could be repaired too, over time. Peter was in a bad way, but Arthur hung up. Ruby and Katie were now his priority, he had woken up to this.

They stepped out into the street, taking a deep breath of relief, as they waited for the police car to come and pick them up. When it did arrive, Dorothy, Colin and Martha stepped out of it and walked silently to their house. The news *THEY* had received was too ghastly for any of them to speak of. Ruby wanted to in some way console them, but she knew she never could. The damage had been done, and who was she to try and repair it?

Nobody had come to visit Peter in hospital. He was glad. Everything felt small and insignificant to him now. Nothingness occupied his mind. Perhaps he should have died at Noble's hands. What was it all in aid of anyway - so many madmen trying to kill him? It had all been ruined for him. Bits of his mind had returned to him, scattering his mentality even more. He felt even more strongly about not returning to his mother now that he could remember her. And then there was Lucy. He had blocked her the most of all. She had been before any of this. Murdered, by unknown hands, forever restless in death awaiting vengeance. Could he carve out a future tracking her killer down? Maybe he had no other option now. He and Lauren would not work out now, not after what had happened with Noble. Yet again something he had tried to create had been spoilt by another. Yet, he realised he had spoilt what she and Noble had going.

He presently looked up at the door, sensing Noose was coming. To his surprise, Noose suddenly appeared moments later, carrying a package. He dawdled some distance from the bed, rubbing his temples.

'I'm not sure what to say to you, Peter.'

Peter smiled. 'I thought you might have come sooner, not that I expected you to come. Nobody else has.'

'Yes. I'm not staying, I just came to bring you this...' Noose stepped up and put the package on the bedside cabinet, stepping away again. He looked out through the window at the car park. It was raining. 'It arrived at Myrtle Mews a couple of days ago.' Peter looked across at the parcel. He just knew it was *I AM DEAD* again. 'We've reached a complete dead-end with the murder investigation.'

'I'm sorry I couldn't have poked my nose in a bit.'

'Hmm. It's going to be a bit of a tarnish on my record, I think. I'll stick at it though, he seemed like a nice enough chap. Misunderstood, shunned, sort of guy.'

Peter laughed, which hurt his jaw. 'I'm gonna go away from here, from everything.'

'Very well,' Noose replied quickly. 'I'm sure...' Noose looked at him, 'I'm sure you'll drift back into all our lives next time YOU just feel like it.' He turned, saying 'Goodbye,' and walked out.

Just beyond the door he met Arthur.

'Did he ask how Katie was?'

Noose just shook his head. Arthur turned and walked out with him.

8PM NEWS: TONIGHT

'Tonight at 10, Peter Smith will commit suicide live on TV and you, the viewers at home, can vote for which method he uses. Still outside the studio where the event is to start broadcasting at 9 is suicide prevention worker Felicity Wood...'

'Thanks Richard.'

'Felicity, earlier tonight we were joined by self-titled pro-suicide campaigner Neville Jeffries, who has since come down to the studio and joined Peter Smith as he prepares for the event. Were you able to speak with Neville in person when he arrived?'

'I was not,' she replies, 'he was driven straight into the studio in a police car.'

'So the police are aiding the event?'

'Yes Richard, with assisted dying now being legal the police are bound by law to protect the safety of all involved. There is no way for suicide prevention campaigners to put a stop to this.'

'Peter is to commit suicide - where does the assisted dying come into play?'

'The fact that the audience can vote for which method Peter uses means they will be assisting him. Richard, I cannot plead enough to both Peter himself and the television studio bosses to put a stop to this vile programme.'

'Thank you, Felicity.' Richard turns from the screen displaying the lone voice in an otherwise heedless herd to look directly into the camera. 'Peter Smith has been courting controversy in the media ever since his arrival in Harnlan nine years ago, quickly becoming a religious and political figure there. The events surrounding his rise have been well-publicised, but what happened in his life before he ended up on the island is also rather intriguing. Reporter Kanak Ollam has been unearthing horrifying cases of multiple murders and suicides stretching back years and all linked to Peter. Perhaps helping give some insight into Peter's present impending action, Kanak has the story…'

'Myrtleville - just your regular, sleepy middle-class town. Peter Smith was born fifteen miles up the road and when he came here, people died. Every time Peter came here there were murders, and suicides. None can be directly linked to the man himself - we are not saying he is a murderer - but the stats are intriguing. The last time he was here, ten years ago, he stayed in this house,' she walks up Myrtle Mews and stops outside Ruby and Arthur's house. 'The family who took Peter in still live here, though they were unwilling to discuss their time with him or how it came to an end. Some of the murders, one of which occurred in this very street, were solved. Some remain unsolved to this day, such as Craig Thompson who was brutally stabbed in his house just up the road. Another was a young woman, Lucy Davies. As a teenager, Peter claimed to have been romantically linked to her, and even stood trial for her murder. One man who stood by Peter during the trial, which eventually saw him acquitted, was Detective Inspector Henry Noose. He too, when asked, was unwilling to discuss Peter Smith with us.' The blinds in Ruby and Arthur's living room window swivel around as a figure lurks behind them, looking out. 'Henry Noose continues to work for Myrtleville Police, despite this list of unsolved murders to his name.'

Kennedy switched the TV off and stood up. A smirk on his face, he walked into the kitchen and poured himself a scotch. Taking a sip, he licked his lips in joy and strolled back through the living room and up the stairs to his bedroom. His wife was long gone, he'd seen to that. His daughter was eleven now. She was sleeping, just in the other room. He put his glass down on his bedside cabinet and leant underneath the bed, pulling a box out. He took the lid off and pulled out the cat mask he'd worn when he killed Craig. Purring, he slipped it on and crawled on all fours to his daughter's bedroom door. He scratched at the door, meowing, purring louder, before pushing the door open and crawling in. She wakened immediately, but kept dead silent. She knew what was coming.

'We're now less than an hour away from the start of the event, where Peter will commit suicide live on TV following a phone-in vote on how to do it,' Richard points out. 'I guess there are two questions on our lips, Felicity,' he continues, turning to face the screen showing her standing outside. 'Firstly, will Peter speak directly to us - marking his first actual public appearance - and secondly, why is he doing this?'

'I can answer both of those questions in one answer - I've no doubt he will be using this stunt of his as a platform to air his pseudo-religious views. We are all playing into his hands.'

'We shall see.' He turns back to the camera. 'And now, we join the regional teams for news in your local area.'

He holds his smile until he goes off-air, before reaching behind a cushion on the sofa and picking up a copy of *I AM DEAD*.

HARNLAN

(NINE YEARS AGO)

ONE

'Do you know what's funny?' Neville asked, one hand clinging onto Peter's shoulder whilst the other clutched his can of lager.

'Your face?' Peter responded, snatching the can off Neville and taking a large gulp from it.

'Good answer,' Neville laughed. 'No, when you got that guy to kiss your shoe in that pub earlier...' Neville smirked. 'Such awesome powers you possess. You could do anything you wished, make anyone do anything by harnessing your connection to The Space, and yet you still have time to use it to do that.'

'And?'

'And yet, it's exactly what I'd do.'

'Would you?' He took another large gulp from the can.

'We're the same, you and me.'

'That's what Noble said.'

'Did he indeed?' Neville laughed again, holding his stomach. Peter crushed the can in his hand and tossed it across the alleyway, shaking Neville's hand off his shoulder and getting to his feet. 'Oh come on, dude! The night's yet young. I tell you what,' Neville continued, he too getting to his feet, 'let's go out round the clubs, get completely hammered and pick up some sluts. What do you reckon?'

'I don't.'

Neville headed after Peter as he made for an industrial-sized bin. 'Come on, we can bring a couple of girls back to our pad.'

'You really think any girls would want to come back here and have sex with us in a bin?' Peter asked his cohort as he climbed into the bin.

'When you put it like that…'

'Anyway, I'm gonna do some reading,' Peter told him, pulling out a wind-up torch from his pocket and whizzing the handle around and around to bring it to life. It shone dimly, but there was enough light for what he wanted to see. 'You coming in or not?' Neville climbed into the bin as well, pulling the lid down. Inside, Peter opened a bag and took out another can of lager, settling down on some rubbish as he opened *I AM DEAD*.

'How far are you?'

Peter showed him. Page 208. Neville chuckled.

'Are things becoming clearer in your mind?'

'Much clearer.' Peter read on, smiling as he did so.

Peter wakened in the morning, giving out a bit of a yawn as he pushed at the weight against his side. It was Neville.

'What a lovely sleep,' Neville uttered without opening his eyes. 'Makes you not want to wake up.'

Peter pushed him off and adjusted his back to a more comfortable position, finding the book in his lap. He had finished reading it last night, and all at once his memories had come flooding out of their dark dungeon like a bad case of diarrhoea. He felt almost complete again, yet burdened with the terrible dread of knowing he had destroyed and recreated everything. Well, he believed he had. He could remember beyond the book, to when he last had all his mind. He had torn down, slaughtered, a bunch of coppers like they were tin cans on top of a fence. But, what had happened beyond that? Why had he been given a second chance? Surely if he was creator of all things he must have given himself a second chance?

He now felt his mind was once again polluted with knowledge of The Space and all its trappings. Throughout the whole time he was reading the book he had the overriding urge to stop, a voice in his head begging him not to go on. But, after nearly dying at Noble's hands, and accepting his death with the bag on his head, he now found an affinity with the book and this spurred him on to read it.

There were lots of voices in his head now, some he recognised as the thoughts of people around him whose minds were open to him. Bland, worthless minds, he reasoned. Other voices, he could not place. He had gone on and finished, the wholeness of his change complete. He had no reason to remain as he had done; Ruby and Arthur had given up on him. Noose too. And, Lauren was beyond the question. He was finished, as was the rest of humanity in his eyes. Could he save them? Save them from what - himself? They had come from him in the first place. They were all as worthless as he felt.

Elder Icon had painted him as a grand figure in the book. A messianic figure. It was he, Peter Smith, who had closed The Space and saved it from ebbing away any further. Love, friendship and respect had all returned. These things were not clear in his mind, though. Who was Elder Icon, and who were these children who followed what she read to them? He still could not fully comprehend The Space either, but felt it was surely that which had shown him the vision of Katie tied up before it had happened. And yet, The Space had closed. If so, it couldn't possibly have shown him that. Then there was Reaping Icon, the one who had set that space by which to goad Peter to placate the sensual. Whatever that meant. He, Peter, was the final link between The Great Collective and The Space. He, and only he, could restore that which had passed. But how? Maybe he had. He had closed The Space. Was that enough? It couldn't possibly be, for this life he had experienced since was not particularly agreeable. In fact, it was utterly awful. He was living in a bin with a madman. This was no place for a great man, he thought. Not just a great man, but The Man. His opinion of himself had inflated rather a lot since reading the book - even if he was an arse in it. That didn't matter. Everybody was an arse. Peter suddenly had a great feeling come over him and he pushed open the lid of the bin. He stood up straight and let the thin slit of light streaming down the alleyway run across his face.

'I'm marvellous!' he called out, raising his hands into the air. 'All this is mine!' he continued, looking up to the heavens. He suddenly dropped down again, a feeling of dread and shame hitting him. 'What am I doing? This isn't right.'

'Oh, it is,' Neville whispered in his ear. Peter leapt up again and jumped out of the bin.

'I'm, I'm Peter Smith. It's all coming back to me.'

'Let it come!'

'Peter! Oh my word!' a voice suddenly squealed from up ahead. Peter turned to look, the light striking him blind as the figure neared in shadow. He turned away, shielding his eyes from the intensity of the beam. 'I knew you could sink to lows, but *THIS* low?'

'Mother?' Peter replied, recognising the voice before he could see her.

'Hah, memory loss, my foot! I knew it was a load of rubbish,' Mother went, coming to her son and grabbing at his clothes to analyse the dirt on them.

'My memory has returned.'

'Has it?' she chuckled, clearly not believing a word he said.

'How did you find me?' he asked, still not able to adjust his eyes to seeing her.

'Your dear brother Stuart tracked you down,' she explained as Stuart stepped from behind her and smiled. 'Living in a bin! Dear lord.'

'The Prosecutor,' Peter responded, Stuart's face being the first to fill his vision as it returned.

'Hi Neville!' Stuart called out happily, waving at him as he poked his head out of the bin.

'How do, my friend?!'

'Wait,' Peter butted in, 'you two know each other?'

'I know everyone,' Neville replied.

'Of course we do,' Stuart explained. 'He was the one who led me to you. We've been liaising for a week or more.'

Peter turned to Neville, agog. 'What are you playing at?'

'Well, here they are, timed with the completion of *I AM DEAD*. Go on, now you can kill them,' Neville chuckled.

'Kill them?' Peter questioned, puzzled. He shook his head. 'No, no, that's not right.'

'Oh Peter,' Mother laughed, 'the man's a tease isn't he. Get a sense of humour. Now,' she pulled him forward, 'you're coming home with us.'

Stuart got behind him and jabbed his finger into his back to send him towards Mother as she marched off. Peter turned back to the bin, where Neville twirled a knife about in his hand. He held it out for Peter, winking. He jumped out of the bin, holding the blade of the knife and outstretching the handle for Peter to take as he followed them. Peter kept looking down at the knife and back up at Neville's suggestive face, pondering what he really wanted to do. He didn't know and wished hard that something would crop up and ensure he did not have to make the decision. That in itself was a decisive decision, as a campervan pulled up at the top of the alleyway and the side door opened.

'You coming?' Darren Aubrey asked Peter, poking his head out with a chef's hat on it. And, Peter recognised him. Not just as The Anarchist who had dealt with Trout and Williams and tied him to a chair in this current existence, he could also remember him from the book. Well, he felt he could remember him. Whether or not his memories were real, or he just thought they were real because he'd read the book, was anybody's guess. He had been so many different shades of the same man in the book; the Judge, The Leader, The Anarchist, The Dealer. Was he still currently The Anarchist?

Neville grabbed hold of Peter's hand and thrust the handle of the knife into it, running forward and hopping into the campervan. 'Finish them off, then we can go.'

'I'm not killing them.'

'Suit yourself.'

The campervan began to pull away, but Peter dropped the knife and leapt forward away from Stuart and Mother and got into it and slammed the door shut just before it sped off.

'We meet again,' Darren gurned as Peter flopped onto the back sofa bed, 'want some beans on toast?' he asked, stirring the contents of a saucepan on the camper stove. The camper turned a corner and went over a bump, splashing some of the beans on his hand. 'Hey, steady old woman,' he exclaimed to the driver as he wiped his hand on his apron.

Peter looked forward to see who was driving, but she was hidden by a curtain pulled across the driver's cabin. Neville slipped through the curtain and sat in the front passenger seat as Peter got up to see who it was. He poked his head through, where an orange sleeve puppet was thrust into his face.

'Well hello there,' it spoke in a strangely deep, rolling voice, 'I'm Mr Monkey. Who are you?' The puppet's purple button eyes took it in turns to protrude, perhaps indicating that they were studying Peter's face.

'I'm Peter Smith.' Peter thought for a second. 'Wait, why am I talking to a puppet?' He looked down at the puppet, but could not decipher who was controlling it. They must have been hidden under the seat or something.

'No need to be rude,' Mr Monkey sighed, turning his back on Peter and looking forward through the windscreen.

Initially drawn away from his purpose, Peter renewed his efforts and turned to see that Gertrude Hinklebottom was at the wheel. Surprised to see Ruby and Arthur's neighbour, Peter at first didn't know what to say.

'What happened to keeping my bush neatly trimmed?' she suddenly demanded, keeping her eyes on the road as the camper hit 75mph.

'Yeah, what about her bush?' Mr Monkey iterated.

'Erm,' Peter thought, 'sorry.' They went over another bump and Darren squealed from the back. 'Look, what the hell is even going on here?' Peter demanded.

'We're off to Harnlan,' Gerty beamed.

'Harnlan?'

'Taking Raymond's ashes.' She tapped an urn, positioned on the dashboard. 'That's where he grew up, before the troubles there of course. Back in the day.' She smiled. 'I think I'm finally ready to let go. Move on.' A tear rolled down her cheek. 'Oh, dear Raymond.'

'Aww bless,' Mr Monkey gabbed sweetly, looking up at her with his button eyes. Peter looked on in disbelief.

Neville reached into his pocket and brought out a little photograph, handing it to Peter. 'Paradise,' he exclaimed, as Peter puzzled over the image of a small island.

'You've never heard of the island Harnlan?' Gerty roared in disbelief.

'Dear me!' Mr Monkey chuckled, shaking his polyester head.

'I've heard of North Harnlan,' Peter mused, passing the photo back to Neville.

'That's on the mainland,' Gerty went on, 'proper Harnlan is south of that.'

'So it's South Harnlan?'

'Well, it WAS. It's officially an island now. Global warming and all the rising sea levels!'

'It's been an island for three months of the year for thousands of years,' Darren called from the back of the camper. 'Rising tide for part of the year.'

'Yes, well now it's four months,' Gerty replied, sulking.

'Soon it'll be all year, every year, and our plan will come to fruition,' Neville smirked.

'Plan? What plan?'

'Enjoy the journey, stretch your mind to The Space. We're gonna be needing your expertise later.'

Peter pulled his head back through the curtains and went to sit at the back of the camper.

'Are you with us yet?' Neville questioned, looming over Peter as he stirred from sleep.

'What?' Peter sat up. 'Yes.'

'No, I mean, are you fully *YOU* again? Now that you've read *I AM DEAD*, see…'

'Of course,' Peter lied, thinking this was his chance to get the upper hand over Neville. And yet, it wasn't that much of a lie. He did feel himself again. But, what exactly was it to feel himself? There seemed no right version to be.

'Good. I have my questions. Why on page 159 do you call Darren's mother Rosetta Harden? There are inconsistencies.'

'Reverting back to her maiden name,' Darren explained, stepping into the camper and opening a cupboard under the sink.

Neville flopped down next to Peter, his head sinking into his hands as Darren picked up a bottle of liquid window cleaner from the cupboard and slammed the door shut. He grinned at the two men as Peter pulled back the curtain in the back window and looked out. They had stopped in a supermarket car park. He could see Gerty and Mr Monkey sitting outside on deckchairs with sunglasses on, her husband's ashes positioned on a foldable camping table between them. She sipped at a glass of orange juice, chatting away to the puppet. Again, Peter strained to see who was controlling Mr Monkey, but he could not see.

'There is much I do not understand, but I want to learn,' Neville continued. 'I *NEED* to learn.'

'It's because he hasn't had sex,' Darren added. 'That's all that this entire thing boils down to. He thinks he can use The Space to lure women into sleeping with him.' He stepped back outside, appearing at the window Peter was looking out of. He sprayed some of the cleaner on it, wiping it around with a rag. Peter dropped the curtain back in place and turned to face Neville.

'Why are you going to Harnlan?' Peter asked.

'We have a plan, you know this. You are back to your old self, are you not? You should know all.'

'Well, yes…' Peter thought. 'But I want to hear it from your lips.'

'It's Darren, isn't it. He'll never change, it's in his nature. Wiping out old people with the dignity experiment, family issues with his parents - everything must repeat itself. Harnlan is merely his current venture, isn't it?'

'I suppose it is.' Grasping for some form of control over Neville, Peter couldn't help feeling he was still missing something. There was something still left blank in his mind, a gap that had yet to be filled. What did indeed happen between recreating the universe and appearing on the bicycle in the country lane? He fought to think, giving himself a headache.

'The big question on *MY* lips,' Neville went, all his usual mystery and humour gone, 'is how we bring you and your gospel to the masses.'

Peter coughed, trying to hide his surprise. He scratched his chin. Neville clearly thought a lot of him. 'Maybe we need to mentally manipulate a top TV executive or some such,' Peter pondered. 'Using The Space, presumably.'

'You think that could be the key?' Neville asked, sitting hunched beside his master.

'Possibly. Or part of the key. In as, getting on TV to manipulate lots of people.'

'Using The Space? You mean to say you have made contact again, despite its closing?'

'Yes,' Peter answered without thought. He *HAD* made contact, he had seen Katie tied up before it had happened. Hadn't he? All his thoughts had rushed back since he'd finished the book. Well, most. Thoughts that had been thought up and actual memories all blurred into one. Peter was unsure, though this did not stop him believing what he thought.

'How would I participate in that, then?' Neville questioned, hunching ever more as Peter's shadow ensconced him when the breeze of the camper door Darren had left open blew the curtain behind him and revealed a flash of sunlight.

'Good question. At present you couldn't, you are simply useless.' Peter smiled, thinking it time he got the upper hand over this mystery man.

'Then I must learn. Question is, how?'

'Not really something that can be learnt in that respect, there has to be something that can be switched on or brought out. You've read *I AM DEAD*, you know this Neville.'

'And how does that happen?'

Peter thought for a second. 'Through many tests and experiments, all of which you have thus far failed.'

'Go on.' Neville urged, the tight clenching of his facial muscles obscured from Peter's vision as he turned his face away just enough. It was just as well.

'Well we've discussed all this at length before.'

'We have?' Neville questioned, shaking his head as his memory failed to pull anything to the fore. 'Surely not? We couldn't have.'

'I know all, Neville, and I know who you really are.' He did not. 'I tell you, we have discussed this before.'

'Very well. Specific tests?' Neville pushed.

'Yes, though asking me to recall specifics will take me time to remember and give adequate details.'

'Well, just one example.'

'You having sex, for one. You have failed to do so and thus failed my test.'

'Ah.' Neville smiled. 'I *KNEW* you were playing at it all, I could tell. You, Peter, have been playing me. Oh this is wondrous, to have *THE* Peter Smith doing this to me. I am truly honoured.' He bowed his head.

'You have also failed to solve *I AM DEAD*, appearing to put absolutely no effort into even trying. Not even understanding the apparent inconsistencies, how foolish!'

'You know how in awe I am of your work, that is not in question. But, surely it is not solely for my benefit. *I AM DEAD*, that is. Plus,' Neville got to his feet, straightening his back, 'let us not forget that it was I who ensured your latest incarnation became aware of the sacred text.'

'Of course. And, let us not forget that *I AM DEAD* has many benefits.'

'I have spent years trying to unearth its depths. Please, award me at least hints as to how to solve its riddles,' Neville begged, desperate. Peter turned his back. 'Maybe that is the key, passing your tests?'

'Perhaps.'

Peter mused about how Neville had first come into possession of the book, and how indeed it had ever been printed in the first place. He strained his mind for the answer, calling out to The Space to reveal it.

'It is destiny to take you to Harnlan,' Neville continued, slipping around Peter to be in his view.

'I see,' Peter laughed. There was so much going on here, and Peter felt he needed a breather. He needed more than that. He further forced his mind in the direction of The Space and sheer torment shot back, slicing his mentality in two. He sought desperately to remain collected in front of Neville, wishing not to recede to his control again.

'Haha. Seriously though, me shagging someone is crucial?'

'Yes. You need to become more human, so to speak. We need to be on a level playing field.'

'And what about you?'

'What about me?'

'Well, are you suggesting you are some kind of Lothario? Your sex-life was always rubbish. If my investigations are correct, you continue to be stilted in your attempts.'

'You have not seen all that I have done.'

'Ah.' Neville sat back down, smiling. 'I often pick up on things, you know. Thinking of saying something myself, deciding not to say it, then someone else will say it instead. Always within about a couple of seconds. And, of course, thinking somebody should do something, then they do it.'

'I see.' Peter now became somewhat worried. Had this conversation turned into something he was not yet prepared to deal with? Who was really in command here - him, or Neville? He could not tell, but felt he must continue to push for control. He had spent a year in this man's company - a man who worshipped him. But, a battle raged on between them. This was a war of mentality. One question from Peter to Neville could collapse his entire army. How did he come into possession of the book?

'Any common things which inhibit spacely function?' Neville continued, eager as a starving dog for a scrap of meat.

'Simply not being talented in that way.'

'I mean less general things.'

'Not really.'

Peter tried to grasp the deep dark recesses of his mind that he did not have conscious access to.

'What about sleep deprivation?'

'Depriving oneself of sleep is very foolish,' Peter reeled off again. 'It leads to false stuff. That which you think is The Space, but is not. Plus, a lot of spacial interaction is easier if you are asleep.' Now a vision slashed at Peter's mind. Neville, a baby in his cot, with *I AM DEAD* by his side. Neville, a young boy just learning how to read, by reading that book. Neville, forever and ever with that book. No beginning, no end, his eternal circle of existence with that book in his possession. Who gave it to him, where did they get it from? There was no answer to be delivered. The infinite paradox.

'Ah. So, might you say that the stuff you get with sleep deprivation is, roughly, comparable to the sort of thing you get with The Space? In terms of what's experienced?' Neville continued without letting up.

'No. Well, what do you experience with sleep deprivation?' Peter was now tiring of this conversation, wishing his mind to go off on a tangent away from Neville. He was a drain, a drain Peter could do without.

'Difficult to describe, but I'll have a go.'

'Mere words do not account for it.'

'It's almost like being right in the middle of a crowded room. You pick up on this or that. Sometimes words, sometimes ideas, but it flits from thing to thing, each one whizzing past. If it's not a string of words, which are sometimes nonsensical, then, as I said, it's more idea or a concept. But the main thing is you can keep with it, listen to it.'

'How odd.'

'Or you can un-tune it and stop.'

'Do you also sniff glue during this period?' Peter snapped, turning away.

'Haha, no. How does that compare?'

'As I say, mere words cannot account for The Space, and interactions with it.'

'Well, you said what you get with sleep deprivation can be confused with The Space.'

'What you are experiencing there is entering the dream world whilst still half-awake. Lucid dreaming. As I said, depriving oneself of sleep is very foolish and leads to false stuff which you think is The Space but is not.'

'I wasn't suggesting it was.'

'You might think it is The Space because you haven't experienced The Space to know the difference,' Peter smirked.

'What I was trying to get was some common point of reference.'

'That is pretty difficult, really. I'm being honest, interacting with The Space is pretty unique and can be different each time. There are also many other things which aren't wholly The Space.'

'Well, do your best to generalise, if you could.'

'Hmm, okay.' Peter sighed. Neville was not letting up, Peter *HAD* to throw him something. 'It's all about perspectives. So, we have you in the middle of this crowded room hearing things. Picking up on this and that from the people isn't The Space, it is The Space allowing you entry into their minds, so it is their mind you are interacting with and not The Space. Get me?'

'Yeah, there's a distinction, using The Space as a hub.'

'So everything you say there about the crowded room is not coming from The Space but the person or people.'

'Or from my own mind - day residue and all that shit.'

'Indeed.'

'So, the distinction between the crowded room and The Space itself-'

'What more is there to say?'

'Well, a more general description of The Space, compared to the crowded room. Interactions with it, loosely speaking.'

'It sounds like *YOU* are the one who needs to read *I AM DEAD.*'

'Yes, yes, visiting an old relative. They either let you in or they don't.'

'But if you're requiring a fresh one, I shall. There is a voice, on occasion, though this can be attributed to the person's voice being used by The Space for communicative purposes. In a way I am uneasy saying too much as previously you have laughed off some things I have said as me personifying The Space etc.'

'Well, you are in a better position to know than I.'

'Of course. I am Almighty. AYE NO ALLLL!'

'Please, continue.'

'Well I dunno what else to say. Short of coming across as a psycho, if that is the right word. Correct me if you wish. I know how you enjoy your fellow man's words.'

'What about the voice?'

'What about it?'

'Who's voice is it?'

'As I say, the person's. Whoever is interacting with The Space.'

'So your own?'

'That is my understanding. The Space uses the voice you have in your head to say things.'

'But not always?'

'Do you suggest another voice, or that a voice is not always used?'

'Well you said there isn't always a voice.'

'I did.'

'If there's no voice, how do things work then?'

'It is delivered as an instinct on occasion. You could say, to drop this to a level somebody of your limited understanding could get to grips with, you are possessed or are overcome with a force which drives you. Say you have an itch on your nose, you scratch it. Same thing. I want or need somebody to do a dance and kiss my shoe - it happens.'

'Interesting. Thing is, can you get information on that instinctive level? Does it work in the other direction too?'

'I can get whatever I wish. You will *KNOW* something about a person. It is delivered to your brain as if by magic.'

'But is it you that invokes it, or is it more passive?'

'What do you mean? You cannot control The Space if that is what you mean.'

'Well, do you have to ask, or is it just provided?'

'Depends what you want the info for. There is the sense of a moral compass.'

'To The Space?'

'The Space appears to have a moral compass.'

'Ah.'

'It would not aid in murder, for example.'

Neville sighed. 'Ever tried to use it for ill?'

'Of course not. I am a wholly moral person.'

Neville narrowed his eyes. 'But it'd aid you in making someone dance around and kiss your shoe?'

'Ah well, now we're talking about residue matter.'

'I see.'

'Harnessing the power given and stretching it out. Anyway, some people are small fish. It is to no long-term detriment if they kiss my shoe. I made that particular individual feel good for doing the act, and you were shown my skills. Win-win. Harnessing the power, for example. This is the residue already around from continued interactions. I rarely have full-on interaction with The Space. Though, it does sometimes show me things. I do, however, harness the residual spaciousness that is blessed to me as the chosen. You could say some of The Space has leaked into me due to prolonged contact. I can achieve things quite easily these days without direct contact.'

'Ah. So for a newbie, how does it begin? Surely there's no residue to begin with?'

'Depends. There are no newbies, so to speak, there are merely those who are not too far gone from prolonged division. You, perhaps, are too far gone. I was saved from an early age and have regained most of what I had from past existences prior to my current life.'

'As I said, I have fleeting things now and again. It's difficult to zero in on.'

'It will be. Let's, for instance, generalise. One of your favourite pastimes, I know. Say I was born with 10% in which to work on. You were born with 0.0001%. Much more watered down. Some might say I have pulled back and stretched myself from 10% to maybe 50 or 60. I intend 100%, which would guarantee full remembrance in future existences.'

'But that, as you say, is after being fully switched on, something which is yet to occur in me.'

'Indeed. Then again, you might think that all I am spouting is mere jolly madness and just messing around between mates. Because, Neville, you and I have grown to be good mates.'

Neville placed a hand on his heart and took a deep breath - breath he noted was being shared with Peter. 'You are neither jolly nor mad. So, one step at a time.'

'Anyway, *I AM DEAD* holds much. There is much fruit to be picked.'

'Yes. I have been looking - looking for a long time.'

'And, it is in the least likely places. Every single word counts. You hold in your hands the word of a genius. However, it *IS* incomplete without the final pieces of the puzzle.'

'What are these final pieces, and how do I unlock them?'

'It is work in progress. We will reap many rewards, but it currently remains incomplete and unpublished.'

'In the meantime I must tup the white ewe.'

'You black ram, you.'

'Is that more important a step than solving *I AM DEAD*?'

'All steps are equal in value.'

'Ah. And we shall speak more after each one?'

'I hope so. It would be nice to have a platonic companion on my immortal journey.'

For Peter, this was a throwaway joke - for Neville, it was an astonishing acceptance from his deity. His entire life had been spent studying the book and trying to gain access to The Space. He was now within reach.

'I have a question for you, please answer it honestly.'

'Go ahead.'

'Do you think I am too far gone?'

'From a desire to avoid your suicide, no.'

'Is that an honest answer?'

'No. I can see how I have come on. It may be possible for you to come on too. However, you have shown basically no development since we've been hanging out. I think you need to overcome many human hurdles before you can progress. In many ways you are a very disturbed man. Maybe The Space does not take kindly to this and is not allowing you access. For, you see, The Space could technically allow anyone access.'

'What human hurdles?'

'You tell me. What does your life lack? What is it that most mentally cripples you?'

'Hmm.'

Unbeknownst to the men, Mr Monkey had been making his way back to the camper a few minutes ago now and, having heard them chatting, had held back just outside the door to eavesdrop on the conversation. 'Blimey!' he exclaimed to himself, shaking his head. 'That's a bit deep, isn't it?!' He pulled his thin lips back as his nose, a strip of black cotton sewn on below the two purple buttons that were his eyes, flexed forth. 'Ooo, ice cream!' And, not bothering to enter the camper after all, headed back around to Gerty where she and Darren were licking the strawberry sauce that had dripped down their ice cream cones.

'You have based your entire life on all this,' Peter continued.

'I have, but it was all fate. It was destiny. I had no choice.'

'Of course not.'

'But, for the first time in my life, I now feel I have a choice. I have the choice to achieve greatness. I decide to choose greatness! But first…' He ushered Peter to move away from the sofa bed. Peter obliged, out of curiosity, and watched as Neville pulled it open to reveal a hidden storage compartment under it. 'I'm finally going to do it!' he beamed as he beckoned Peter to look down into the storage space beneath where he had just been sitting. Peter looked in and saw Sharon inside, naked and with her legs and arms bound. Her eyes were open, and they slowly moved about a bit, but whether or not they were actually seeing anything was another matter. 'I'm finally going to lose my virginity!' Neville chuckled.

TWO

The journey was well and truly underway, and it was time for yet another stop.

'You're bloody useless, you are!' Gerty grunted at Darren, who had just narrowly missed pushing her into a wall. 'You're about as straight as a roundabout.'

'Oh shut up you stupid old bitch,' he shot back, letting the wheelchair go and storming off in the opposite direction.

'Don't be like that! What am I going to do now?' she asked her helper, clutching desperately onto Raymond's urn.

'Why don't you ask Mr Monkey to push you?' Darren yelled back as he disappeared down the hallway.

Gerty growled, stepping out of the wheelchair and pushing it down the hallway herself. She reached a door with a nametag on it reading "Ethel Hinklebottom". She took a deep breath, letting go of the wheelchair, and slowly opened the door with one hand as she held tightly onto the urn with the other.

'Mother?' she called out in a whisper.

'Her tits are a bit saggy, gonna fall into her armpits when I'm bonking her,' Neville explained as Peter mused over the morality of the endeavour, 'and her teeth could do with sprucing up a bit, but hey, beggars can't be choosers can they?!'

'This is how you plan on dealing with your sex issue?' Peter asked the bizarre man, who just smiled in response. Peter leant over and looked through the window of the camper at the nursing home across the way.

'They cremate them here too,' Neville remarked as Peter looked across at a small concrete building with a chimney billowing out black smoke.

'I suppose you've come to smother me,' the ancient woman whispered from her bed. She was not whispering purposely, her voice was just that way. So many years of existence does that. 'Just like you smothered Raymond.'

'Oh Mother!' Gerty giggled back, sitting next to her mother's bed.

'Take pity on me,' Ethel pleaded, managing to clutch onto her daughter's wrinkly hand with her even more creased claw. 'Do me in, please. Life isn't worth living.'

'But Mother, there's a lot to live for. TV?'

'All I can see is fog. My eyes are shitty.' She coughed.

'That's because your glasses are dirty.'

'There isn't even any pleasure in getting rescued from the bath in here. At home, I had those hunky firemen coming and getting me. All you get here is a fatty matron.' Her eyes flicked towards the window. Some of the light struggled through her foggy vision and brought a glimmer of a smile to her face. 'I've lived long enough.'

'I suppose you have,' Gerty mused. 'I certainly don't want to live to 108.'

'Nor would I advise it.' She let go of her daughter and struggled to pull the pillow from under her head. It dropped to the floor. 'Oh go on, Gerty, you were always such a good girl to me, not like that naughty boy Bertram!' A tear rolled down her cheek. 'Oh, Bertram! Nobody wants to outlive their own child.'

Gerty bent down and picked the pillow up, clutching it in her hands. 'Raymond was ever so ill, Mother,' she cried gently, looking down at the urn in her lap. 'It was better that he slipped away when he did.'

'Do me the same favour, my girl,' Ethel pushed, 'assist me. Give me dignity!'

Darren kept on storming, but suddenly stopped when one door caught his attention. He looked down at the name on it. The surname caught his eye. "Warrender". All those childhood memories resurfaced as he took the name in.

Darren, just a child, looked up at Mr Warrender, who leant as far in as his humongous stomach would allow.

'I am omnipotent,' he spat at the boy, 'You are expedient.'

Next he was in a horrible room in almost pitch darkness, a huge four poster bed his only companion. Darren could remember looking through the window at the bright moon. He thought how bright it was even though it was just dead. So bright and so dead.

'To remain silent and unseen is your life's work from this day forth,' the obese man shouted at the young boy, slamming the door shut. Darkness.

'Memories,' a voice announced beside Darren in the hallway. He turned and came face to face with Reaping Icon, who smiled. Darren's brow creased. 'You know me, don't you?'

'Yes,' Darren replied, instantly recognising the figure but not fully knowing where from. Again, Darren's mind was full of Mr Warrender and the time he spent in his "care":

Mr Warrender was in his study, searching for a book on a high shelf. Finding what appeared to be an ancient tome, he removed it from the shelf and walked back to his desk, flopping down on his chair. An open fire flickered in the background. Burning and burning.

Positioning the book in the centre of the desk, he carefully opened it. The book had been hollowed out, becoming a storage for pornographic magazines. He looked down at them - sweating, grinning - preparing to gently remove the top one from its protective sheath. But, he paused, looking up from his desk. There stood the young Darren, eyeing the books up on the plethora of shelves. Lines and lines of tomes.

'Old age doesn't come by itself,' Mr Warrender announced rhetorically, coughing, closing the book. 'My eyesight fails me. My books go unread.' He struggled to his feet, carrying the book back to its original position on the shelf. Darren picked a book up. 'You are not to come in here again,' Mr Warrender snarled, snatching the book off the boy.

But, Darren went back to the study later. He approached the book case, stepping up onto one of the shelves to reach a higher book - the ancient tome sheathing those porn mags. He pulled it down.

Placing the book on the floor, he opened the cover. Staring up at him was an older boy's dream. This young boy's eyes widened. He picked the magazine up.

'They warned me about you,' a voice uttered. Darren turned and looked up at Mr Warrender's desk. The chair spun around, the big fat old man sitting upon it. He stood up. 'What could I do? I'd promised your grandmother.' He approached Darren, who ran for the door, but the old fat man quickly blocked it. He picked him up and lifted him into the air by his curls, snatching the magazine from his stumpy fingers. 'Why were you reading such filth? How did you get hold of it?' he yelled at Darren, who stared blankly back. 'No more will your eyes feast upon such fancies.' He tossed the magazine into the open fire. It burned and burned. 'There's only one way to deal with naughty boys like you.' He threw him to the floor and pulled his trousers down. 'This is the only way.'

Suddenly the old house was ablaze. Firemen tried desperately to fight off the raging inferno as Darren, but a boy, looked on, smiling.

Reaping Icon just nodded, having shared in Darren's past glimpse, and looked at the door leading to Mr Warrender. Darren opened it and stepped in. Facing him in the room was the back of an armchair, a bulbous figure housed in it. He walked slowly around to face the man.

'Where the hell have you been? Shat myself an hour ago, been sat in my own bloody filth,' the old man shouted out, looking up at Darren and squinting. 'Wait a second, who are you?'

Darren tried to smile, but couldn't. All he could do was look down at the burn scars upon the old man's face. Scars *HE* had caused all those years ago. And yet, here was this man still alive.

'Bad people always live too long,' Darren responded. Mr Warrender's eyes widened as he recognised who this was in front of him.

'Come to finish the job, boy?'

Darren looked down at a half-finished dinner on a table in front of the old man. The knife, in particular, seized his attention most. He shivered momentarily, desperate to get out of there. He moved back towards the door, where Reaping Icon was still standing. Darren looked right at Reaping Icon, who nodded again and raised his eyebrows as if to look sympathetic. This was enough to persuade Darren to spin back around, grab the knife from behind the armchair and drag it across Mr Warrender's neck. As the thick blood slipped out between the long slit, Darren paused and thought he had finished. Suddenly, however, something came over him and he went into a frenzy, hacking at the poor git's neck and head. Eventually the limp body flopped forward, prompting Darren to jump on top and pull at the loose head. It came off and free in his hands as the rest of the body pushed the dinner leftovers aside and slammed to the floor.

Darren turned the head around to look at the face, the sunken eyes only just having ceased to see. He thought about

Mr Warrender's last image, a pair of curtains pulled untidily across the window even though it was light outside. Rather curious. He remembered the old man having done the same back in the day. Had he been hiding from something? Now Darren felt an immense avalanche of dread pour down upon himself, almost like Mr Warrender's woes had immediately become his own.

'What are you after?' Darren asked the head.

'Just a kiss,' it replied. Darren lifted it to his mouth and kissed at the old dead lips.

'Was that all you ever wanted from me? Did I not allow you what you wanted?'

He tossed the head on the floor and one of the eyes winked at him. He ran at it, kicking it against the wall repeatedly until it had splattered about the place. His shoe, sodden with gore, squelched as he limped from the room. But, seeing Reaping Icon once more in the door, he turned back to the corpse on the floor and pulled at the trousers, tearing them and the underpants underneath them off. Greeting his nostrils first was the stench of Mr Warrender's diarrhoea, the sight of it quickly following for Darren's senses to digest. Now he dropped his own trousers, pulling his penis out. About to get down, his mouth suddenly filled with vomit and he coughed it down onto the body. What the *HELL* was he doing? He pulled his trousers back up, turning back to face Reaping Icon, bounding towards him and out of the room.

Peter had left the camper, and Neville pulled the curtains to in anticipation of what he had planned now that he was alone with Sharon. He pulled her out of her hiding place and dumped her on the floor, setting up the sofa bed to accommodate them both. She, silent, moved her eyes slowly up towards Neville. He leant in, grinning at her and licking his lips, as he picked her up and dropped her on the bed. Undoing her hands, he separated them and went about re-tying each one to a window handle either side of the camper. And then, most importantly, he bent down and slowly undid the string around her legs, all the time a little too nervous to look directly between them at his ultimate desire.

Shaking, he pulled the legs apart and stole a glance at the vagina. There it was, waiting for what he intended for it. Initially he folded his arms, rubbing his lips, and raised an eyebrow.

'Oh dear, oh dear,' he sighed, 'I'm ever so nervous.'

Her head, tossed to one side, slowly rolled to the other side as she tried to close her gaping mouth.

Slowly, Neville removed his clothing. Firstly, his plain white t-shirt came off and he laid it on the little camper table, folding both arms to the centre, followed by the left side to the right, and the bottom to the top. Barely able to undo his belt with the shakes, he clung onto his trousers and pulled them down, lifting each leg out as slowly as he could. Again, he placed them on the little table and folded them as many times as he could. Next, he analysed his underpants. There was a little button on the front of them, and Neville contained himself long enough to undo this. Popping his flaccid penis through the slit that the button had held together, he took a gulp and turned to Sharon. He looked down again, his white socks pulled right up as high as they could get, as his penis curled to one side. He took the one little step needed to reach the foot of the camper bed where Sharon lay, tied up and naked, waiting. He put his knees on the bed in between her spread legs and rested his weight on them, leaning down over her, gingerly placing his hand on one of her breasts and pushing at it, moving it about a bit.

His nostrils caught a whiff of something, and he jumped up away from her. Keen to think it himself and not her, he confidently pulled his foreskin back and rubbed his finger along the skin under it, bringing it up to his nostrils to investigate. Sufficiently repulsed, he opened the slim little door leading into the camper shower and quickly removed his underpants and socks.

'Back in a jiffy!' he told his lady friend, turning the shower on and stepping in.

Gerty removed the pillow from her mother's face just as Peter poked his head around the door.

'Did you just smother her?' he asked.

'Smother my own mother? Preposterous!' she replied.

'These old farts, they're small fry,' Reaping Icon told Darren as they exited the building. 'Peter Smith is the oldest of the lot, older than the universe itself. You must kill him, surely?'

'I am also important,' Darren responded.

'Yes, you are! In fact, you are the most important of all.'

'But I can't hear The Space any longer, not like I could in the book.'

'He who kills Peter Smith usurps his link to The Space,' Reaping Icon pointed out.

'I will hear it again if I do him in?'

'Not only will you hear it, you'll control it. The Space will be at your whim.' Reaping Icon raised his hand up into the air and, almost about to grasp hold of something only he could see, suddenly lowered it to his face and checked his nails. 'Humanity.'

'I can instil my will onto the masses?'

'You can destroy the universe!'

'Tempting.'

Darren burst into the camper, expecting to find Peter waiting to be destroyed. Instead, he found Sharon. Bemused, he turned and shut the door, wondering what to do. Although not the grandest beauty in the world, Sharon's body was nonetheless pleasing enough to garner Darren's attention. He was, after all, unscrupulous when it came to this sort of thing. He quickly tore his clothes off and got on top of her, grabbing hold of her head and thrusting his penis into her mouth. He laughed as he pounded at her limp head, thinking it his lucky day. Choking on this dreaded thing in her mouth, she came to life and tried to pull away. He kept at it, so she bit down as hard as she could, driving her incisors deep into his shaft. His face contorted in terror and torment as he punched and punched at her face to get her to stop. Only would she stop when she'd got through the whole thing, and Darren stumbled off her with no penis anymore.

She, penis in mouth, couldn't get it out, and no amount of coughing seemed to help. Her face swelled a brilliant violet, contorting into a myriad of complex shapes as she attempted to dislodge the object. Almost near death, she somehow found the right jaw movement to get rid of the by now flimsy member and it propelled into the air, landing with a plop on the camper floor as Neville opened the shower door to see what was going on. She gasped in joy at survival, and started to become aware of what was going on around her. She looked across at her "victim", as a naked Neville picked up the penis.

'Does this belong to you?' he asked Darren, waving it about.

Suddenly the driver's door opened and Gerty got in, followed by Peter through the passenger door. She started the engine up and was pulling away as she noticed what was going on.

'For goodness sake, where's all that blood from? You'll ruin the carpet,' she yelled.

'My penis, my penis!' Darren cried out, looking at it in Neville's hand.

'Looks like my girlfriend bit it off. How did that happen, eh?' asked Neville angrily. 'You weren't fiddling about with her, were you?'

'If you lay down with dogs, you're going to get up with fleas,' was Gerty's quip on the matter.

'Oh God, you need to get me to a hospital quick,' Darren went on.

'Nonsense!' Gerty exclaimed. 'I was a nurse, I can deal with this. First thing's first, we need to get away from this place. When we are, we'll pull up and sort you out. What do you say to that?'

Darren struggled to his feet and was thrown to one side as the camper turned a sharp corner. He made a grab for Sharon, but Neville pulled him away, slapping him across the face with the penis.

'I say we cook it,' Neville laughed as Darren rolled about on the floor.

'Don't be silly,' Gerty replied calmly, 'I can sow it back on. I was top embroiderer in my class at school.' She smiled through the rear view mirror. 'This is all in hand. Fear not.'

Peter looked around. 'Where's Mr Monkey?'

A hand appeared, upright, the thumb pressed under the four fingers to make a jaw. 'I'm just popping in the shower whilst it's running,' Mr Monkey's voice spoke out as the hand moved in tandem with the words, before disappearing again.

'It *IS* a problem,' Gerty mused, looking across at Sharon from the driver's seat. She had spun it around, pulling the cabin curtain open, and now surveyed the mess. Sharon was still naked and bound. 'We could all be implicated in a kidnap.' She tapped her chin. 'I suppose I could act as a mother hen in a ladies prison.' She sipped at her mug of coffee.

'Prison? Yippee!' Neville cut in, doing a little tap dance of joy. The camper rocked slightly, and a stern look from Gerty was enough to discourage him from further outbursts of happiness.

'Gerty, darlin', how have I ended up here?' asked the bruised prisoner, her jaw sore with having removed Darren's penis. She had since pulled her legs together, and they lay tightly wrapped up on the bed.

'Deary me, this is an unfortunate situation. We might have to kill her,' Gerty chewed, munching on a biscuit at the same time. Sharon burst into hysterical screaming, which sent Neville cowering under the table with his hands pawing at his ears. 'My silly dear, nobody will hear you here. We've pulled up in the middle of nowhere.' Sharon ceased, but probably more from vocal exhaustion than Gerty's words.

Darren, lying slumped against the opened shower door, vomited into the portable potty. He couldn't quite believe what had befallen him. He had come to slay Peter, and usurp his link to The Space, but instead had had his penis bitten off. Now he lay bleeding to death, an old woman denying him his pleads to be taken to hospital. He wanted life, he desperately wanted life. The only reason he wanted life, though, was to end other lives. He had just done so, and perhaps this was his payment. Why was Reaping Icon not assisting him now? Had Reaping Icon ever assisted him? It seemed like all he had done was goad him into placating that which pleased him, that which he found sensual. He had indeed found it a sensual thrill to kill Mr Warrender, but now he regretted it. Would he have regretted it if he still had his penis and had also managed to kill Peter? Who knows. That question would never be answered. Many questions would now never be answered. He felt himself slipping away, his vision darkening around the edges, as Gerty hobbled towards him, pulling a rubber glove onto each hand. Peter threaded a needle with some cotton as Neville passed Gerty an awful looking red thing in a sandwich bag. Darren knew that was his penis, though it had become a vile lump of decaying flesh. Maybe it had always been vile. He had committed untold horrors with it, in all the lives he could recall having lived. This was his penance, he deserved it. Reaping Icon had goaded him to placate the sensual, and he had paid the price.

Peter was invincible. Not one of Reaping Icon's collection could bring him down. All four - Tony, Jim, Stephen and Darren - had failed. But, Reaping Icon knew everything that had ever or would ever occur. Surely he knew they would all fail and Peter would continue to live? Maybe that was the point.

Gerty drove the needle into the blood-soaked floppy stump above Darren's saggy scrotum and got no response to the pain. He had slipped into unconsciousness.

'Hmm,' she thought, getting up and opening the back camper door. She looked out onto the vast mountains ahead, a valley beneath them. 'He's had it. He always was a rotter, shouldn't have done that to Sharon should he.' She turned and pulled at one of his feet. 'Come on, you two,' she told Peter and Neville, who helped her drag him out. They struggled outside with him, tossing him down into the valley. His body gained considerable speed, the various brambles and wild rosebushes tearing him to shreds. Eventually he came to rest at the bottom, his face submerged in an inch trickle of brown water, where he died.

Peter knew Darren had died, for all at once his memory was filled with everything that ever was or ever could be. That everything was nothing was now fulfilled, Peter knowing full well who Reaping Icon was. And, he knew he had tried to escape the inevitable so many times before, but each time things just reverted back to how they had to be. There was now nothing left of the potential for pure goodness that Noose could see in Peter. No, it was now pure evil. Then again, was there much difference? It was all a matter of opinion, after all.

'I need a wee,' Sharon called, before doing it right then and there. Some of the urine ran down her leg whilst the rest stained the bed.

THREE

'Do you wipe your bum sitting down or standing up?' a tired Alex asked Katie and Emma in the back of the camper.

'Why are you even asking that?' Katie sighed back, rolling her eyes.

They were hurtling down the road, with Arthur at the helm of this battered old thing and Ruby sitting loyally by his side. The kiddies were in the back, disregarding any requirements to strap in, and freely bounced and rolled about. Well, perhaps not quite bouncing and rolling. There was an air of frustration amongst the threesome that went beyond the blame of their current confines in the vehicle. Something else was going on, something that all three were not altogether privy to. It was a matter of need-to-know. It was a matter of keeping quiet, something Emma wasn't really happy with doing. She and Alex eyed each other up with mild contempt. He wanted desperately to keep what happened between them from Katie, but she wanted to tell her friend. He also wanted to get his penis into a girl's mouth again - preferably Katie's. He wanted everything from, and of, her - yet felt he had had nothing. She kept that which he desired just out of his grasp, flaunting it in front of his eyes every waking moment.

'You're supposed to wipe it sitting down,' Ruby called out from the front.

'Why?' Arthur questioned, awe and trepidation fusing to force out a feeling of mild dismay.

'You get it cleaner then, 'cause the cheeks are more spread apart.'

'You mean to tell me I've been making a fundamental hygiene error for basically half a century?' Arthur cried back in amused horror.

'One of many errors, Arthur, one of many,' Ruby laughed back as Katie stared out of the window at the rushing trees on the other side of the road. In times gone by she may well have either buried her head in her hands, or entered into the discussion in a tirade of verbal insults. Not now. Alex turned away, gritting his teeth.

'What I've always wanted to know is how astronauts go to the toilet in space,' Arthur waxed. 'Surely up there it would all just float about.' Ignored, he sighed.

'I just wanted to lighten the mood, that's all,' Alex mumbled under his breath.

'That's your idea of fun, is it - talking about wiping your arse?' Katie suddenly shouted back. He wasn't taken aback by her outburst, he'd had it before. In fact, he'd had it quite a lot from her recently. That was all he'd been getting from her, and this was what was frustrating him. But, what was frustrating her? If only she'd let go sometimes, he thought, and give herself over to her repressed sexual desires - if, indeed, they featured him. He simply didn't know.

'Look, will you lot give over,' Ruby cut in, 'I've been looking forward to this holiday for months, and you lot ain't gonna spoil it for me.'

'You look forward to sleeping in a van?' Katie questioned, shaking her head.

'After what happened last year I thought you'd be pleased with a holiday,' Emma pointed out, to no response from her friend.

'She's not pleased with anything these days,' Alex remarked, turning his back on the pair. Katie's breathing deepened as she turned to stare intently at the back of Alex's head. Perhaps she was envisaging herself putting a knife in it?

'Hey look,' Ruby called out, pointing at a camper parked up on the side of the road. 'Isn't that Gerty?' Both she and Arthur squinted ahead at the figure of their elderly neighbour sitting at the side of the van on a deck chair, a mouth full of cake occupying her attention.

'Well blow me!' Arthur exclaimed. Alex sniffed and raised an eyebrow, perhaps likening Arthur's words to something else.

'Pull over,' Ruby demanded as they neared. Arthur did so, coming to a halt just a few metres behind.

'We've got company,' Gerty called back through the open camper door. Neville poked his head out of the door for a quick look before slamming it shut. Inside, Peter peeped through the drawn curtains at the back and recoiled upon the sight of Ruby and Arthur stepping out of their vehicle. Sharon struggled for a look, but Peter easily pulled her away from the window and pushed her down. She couldn't resist, for her hands and feet were bound.

'Shush,' Peter whispered, placing his finger on her lips. She stared intently into his hypnotic eyes as he began gently caressing her rough cheek. 'You're beautiful,' he went on, moving closer to the shaking nude, 'in your way.' She stayed silent, unable to break contact with him. Neville too, though burning with rage at the sight of Peter usurping his chosen woman, could not move in and stop what was unfolding. Peter now held all of The Space's might in the palm of his hand, and he could do whatever he wished with it. And then, he pulled away from Sharon and realised he was still but a man, unable to face Ruby and Arthur. Here he was, cowering in a camper van, just feet away from the family he had almost managed to call his own. He had made a mess of that, and now slipped ever further and further into murderous deliriousness.

The sudden presence of his surrogate parents at this time of dark fulfilment served only to shatter Peter's delusions of grandeur. He was complete in his power, yes, but to what end? He had nothing. What good that had brought him had been taken by some inert corruption which he could not escape. Thus, he had embraced the corruption and become what he had always presumed he would end up being. There was no way back now. He was heading down a never ending slope of murder and manipulation with Neville for no worthy purpose.

Meanwhile outside, Gerty continued to fill her mouth with cake. 'Well, well, well, what a coincidence,' she spat through the mouthfuls. 'I'm eating it before Mr Monkey catches sight of it!' she remarked, packing yet more cake into her mouth as Ruby and Arthur looked on, hungry.

'Mr Monkey? Blimey, have you still got that?' Arthur laughed.

'*THAT*?' Gerty cried indignantly.

'Yeah, that puppet you used to scare all the kids with.'

The old woman looked off into the distance, at the endless forest ahead, lost in loneliness and regret. Why exactly did she never have any children? She had wanted them. Sometimes, these things just don't happen.

'So what brings you this far from home?' Ruby asked her sharply.

'I need to stretch my legs,' Alex announced, opening the door to step out. He gave Emma a long, hard stare as if to warn her not to say anything foolish to Katie, before departing. Emma got up too and followed him out. She took a moment to get her bearings, spotting Alex making his way behind a tree across the road. Though he was moving fast, it didn't take long to catch up with him and she called out for his attention. He kept on moving, lost in sexual frustration.

'Alex!' she called again, putting her hand on his shoulder. He pulled away from her and carried on moving. 'Where are you going?'

'I need some space... to think.'

'It's like a maze in here. Don't get lost.'

He stopped and turned to face her. 'I can't keep on like this, you're holding me to ransom.'

'What do you mean?'

'All you keep saying is that you're gonna tell Katie about what we did, then you don't go through with it. You're driving me mad.'

'Be with me,' she cried out.

'Keep your voice down,' was his response, as he turned to move further into the forest. There were now many trees between them and any other signs of civilisation up on the road. Alex stopped again, and glanced at the bark on one of the vast oaks. 'There's Katie, it's messy.'

'She's frigid. She won't do anything.' She stepped up close, but he kept his back to her. She put her arm around his body and reached down to his trousers, undoing the flies and slipping her fingers inside. She felt his penis harden and he did not resist as she pulled it out and masturbated him. He held onto the tree with both hands, shafting his body back and forth as she pulled ever harder and faster on him. Finally, with a grunt, he finished, and bowed his head in shame. She paused for a moment, thinking he would turn around. He did not. Hurt, she turned and walked away, wiping her hand on a tree as she passed it.

'Yes, lovely and peaceful here, isn't it?' Arthur rolled as he sat down next to Gerty. Ruby reappeared from the side of their camper with a big hamper and plonked it down in front of the pair.

'It's delightful that you and I have settled our differences, Ruby,' Gerty went, the slightest sign of tears forming. 'There was a time when we couldn't have set eyes on each other without giving it what for.'

'Things have changed, Gerty. I've come to realise how precious life is and how trivial such bickering is,' Ruby replied.

'Yes, you're right.' The old woman felt overwhelmed with guilt at all her dodgy dealings over the years. She had been a crook, there was no doubt about it. Was it too late to turn over a new leaf?

Emma came back from within the trees and walked back to the camper.

'Coming to join us?' Ruby called over to her.

'Erm,' she responded, seeing that Katie had not done so. 'No, I'd better check on Moody.' With a nod from Ruby, she carried on and slowly entered the vehicle. Closing the door, she kept her back to her friend, who was sitting on the sofa looking out of the window. Emma felt sure she and Alex had been too far into the forest to have been spotted.

'What happened?' Katie quietly asked her best friend.

'What do you mean, what happened? Nothing happened,' the guilty party responded.

'So you didn't catch up with him then?'

'No.'

Emma slowly turned sideways to catch a glimpse of Katie's face. It was not registering any out of the ordinary emotions. Not yet. Satisfied her friend knew nothing, Emma moved and sat down beside her.

'It's amazing what can happen in life,' Katie blurted out. 'One minute it's all in one direction, then something happens and it's heading in the other direction.'

'You could say that,' Emma replied, fidgeting.

'I don't want to go out with him anymore.'

Emma found herself only half-surprised by this revelation. 'Oh, and why's that?' She felt Katie's hand come and rest on hers.

'I don't know. It doesn't feel right.'

Emma looked at Katie, who was looking right back at her. Katie's hand gripped Emma's tighter, and the two somehow mutually leant in and shared a kiss. They both pulled back again, unsure who had initiated it. Katie felt she had, her cheeks reddening in shame. But, Emma moved in for another kiss. This time it was passionate, their wet tongues sloshing and slapping about in each others mouths. Emma pulled her hand away from Katie's and instead placed it on her leg, rubbing hard at her thigh. Katie's breathing deepened, her eyes unable to fully open as Emma moved her hand up Katie's skirt and rubbed between her legs through her tights. Emma was unsure why she was even doing this, only that it seemed to be what her friend wanted.

'Is this what you want?' Emma whispered in Katie's ear as she kissed her neck. Katie, experiencing her first ever arousal, nodded as her lips pursed. 'Somebody might walk in on us.'

Katie was unable to respond, and Emma's fingers moved up above the tights and slid down against the smooth skin under the tights and knickers to the moist vagina within. Emma had only ever felt her own, but thought how similar this felt to hers. That made her reason that this felt right, and she ran her finger up and down between the lips as Katie gave out a gasp as her legs spasmed and her cheeks tensed. Emma pushed her finger inside just as the camper door opened. Quickly she leapt away from Katie, who collapsed in a fit of ecstasy.

'What's the matter?' Alex asked his girlfriend, having just missed the scene by a nanosecond. She, unable or unwilling to respond, just didn't reply to him, and that was that.

Neville looked down in wonder at Sharon as she looked longingly up at Peter, who had his back to the pair.

'Can you not somehow transfer her desire for you onto me?' Neville almost pleaded, disguising his request as a mere interesting hypothesis.

'I can do as I wish,' Peter responded, and suddenly Sharon looked at Neville with the same facial expression. 'And now, you can do as you wish. Untie her and see.'

Neville did so, and she put her arms around the man.

'Oh God!' Neville exclaimed, wetting himself.

'Yes?' asked Peter.

Peter turned to face them both, but could not see them. He saw only Reaping Icon, who grinned at him and said: 'And if we were to sum it all up, we'd have to say this: everything is nothing. That was, is and will be the key to this, and that and It. It was simply that - nothing. Nothing all along. You are nothing, I am nothing. We are nothing. We are the same. I am you and you are me. I am the culmination of everything you ever were, are and will be. We are nothing. And then again, what is nothing? Nothing is just that, the summation of everything. It all. It is the circle of things, the circle of everything as nothing. Everything *IS* nothing, and saying that is hilarious. Your life is everything to you, and it is nothing to me. And, I *AM* you.' Peter could not reply to Reaping Icon. To *HIMSELF*.

'Yes, but what is It?' Neville asked, as though he had heard Reaping Icon. Had he?

'It is-' Reaping Icon paused, suddenly breathless, clutching onto his chest. 'It is...' He dropped to his knees. 'It is coming.' He flopped forward, slamming onto the floor. Neville knelt over him, pondering whether to check for a pulse.

'Maybe It has already arrived!' Neville responded glibly, rolling the corpse over with his foot. Reaping Icon's face was strangely pleasant now, and Peter could see it was his own. But, there was no time to waste here looking down upon it any longer. There were things to do, weren't there? It had to be done. A cool beat came from up ahead, nearing. It caught the two men, who started nodding their heads and tapping their feet. They were joined by others - all those they had ever known in their lives - as they launched into a full-scale jive to the tune. The band floated up and past them on a huge platform, the music and dancers fading before once more only the two men were left again. Neville looked through Peter. He could not see him there any more. Peter tried dancing alone, but felt very self-conscious. With nobody else dancing along he felt he was the only one being watched. Watched by nothing. Nothing was always there, but came to the fore when everything else was not. And everything was nothing. And Reaping Icon wanted It.

Reaping Icon got up off the floor and burst into fits of hysterical laughter. 'YOU!' he screamed at Peter, thumping his own head with both fists. Suddenly he was gone, and Peter just saw Neville and Sharon again. They were kissing and caressing each other. Peter left them to it, stepping into the bathroom and sliding the lock shut.

'Well, it was nice catching up Gerty, but we must be getting on,' Ruby announced, stretching her legs. Arthur appeared to have fallen asleep, so a sharp prod from his better half was necessary to rouse him. He struggled to his feet, yawning.

'Be seeing you,' Gerty replied, unable to smile. She had much to think about.

They got back in their van and drove off. Gerty gave a half wave, getting to her feet and ambling across the road towards the trees. As she looked through them at the wilderness within, Mr Monkey appeared by her side.

'Ah,' he sighed. 'Life!'

'Too true, Mr Monkey, too true.' She too sighed, rubbing her arm. 'Where did it all go so wrong, eh?' she suddenly asked her companion. His tatty orange polyester fur seemed brighter than normal as it glistened in the evening sun.

'Was it ever right to begin with?' he fired back, full of mischief.

'Oh it was,' she mused, 'back in my youth - before others polluted me. I remember the good old days on the farm, raspberry-picking 'til the cows came home. Those certainly were the days. Mother found it hard after Father died, of course. Things changed when Uncle Freddie came to live with us. I could have lead such a good life, but I didn't.'

'Well, nobody is perfect are they? Look at me! I've been arrested for going ape-shit on nine separate occasions,' the puppet replied, chuckling.

'People do snap, Mr Monkey. It's the way of things now, the way we all live. It's all gone to pot.'

'That's the way it must be, I suppose.'

'No! There *MUST* be change! You and I, Mr Monkey, we must right the wrongs we have done in our lives. We must make up for our misdeeds by doing good deeds.'

'Must we?' he sighed.

'Indeed! From this day forth, we shall put right what is wrong! If ever someone needs our help, or we see wrong being done, we will do all we can to assist.'

She waved her fist in the air as Mr Monkey made various unreadable facial expressions.

'What are you doing in there?' Neville called out to Peter, banging on the door. There was no response. Again he tried to rouse his idol. Nothing. He pushed and pulled at the door with a mighty, manic strength, and worked it open. Out dropped Peter onto the camper floor, with his penis still loosely in his palm and a plastic bag tightly sealed over his head. He was dead, and Neville choked in horror and anguish. He tore the bag off Peter's head, which had gone black.

Pushing the camper door open, Neville instructed Sharon to help him carry the body out. They looked around, catching sight of Gerty and Mr Monkey in the distance. They did not catch sight back. Tossing the body down into the forest, Neville grabbed hold of Sharon and pulled her down towards it. They both slipped, and found themselves tumbling down at equal speed to Peter's corpse. Eventually all three came to a halt, and Sharon watched in obedient awe as Neville flipped open his penknife and cut Peter's face off. He pulled the skin from the skull and placed it over his own face.

'I'm Peter now!' Neville roared. Disturbed by an engine, they looked up to see the campervan driving off. Gerty and Mr Monkey had ditched them. Neville turned back to Peter and placed a hand on his chest, still holding his face in his other hand. He felt something in Peter's breast pocket and pulled it out. It was a notebook. On the front cover was scrawled: *THE MUSEUM CLUB MURDERS*. 'Pieces to the puzzle,' Neville screamed with joy, jumping to his feet and raising the notepad into the air. Suddenly he panicked, thinking about *I AM DEAD*. Quickly he searched Peter's body. To his dismay he could not find it. He turned back to the disappearing camper, only to spot something tossed out of the passenger window. He galloped back up to the road, still clinging onto Peter's face, and saw the tattered book lying strewn in the middle of the road up ahead.

FOUR

Sharon lay sprawled in the middle of the road. Unmoving, it seemed to all who may have clapped eyes on her that she was dead. A car came speeding along the lonely stretch towards her, screeching to a halt. A man jumped out, running to her aid. He got as far as checking for a pulse before Neville appeared behind him with a rock, slamming it down onto his head. The man dropped to the ground, and Sharon came to life. She and Neville carried the man to the car, tossing him in the boot, and drove off.

'Harnlan, here we come!' he laughed, forcing the car to the limits of its power.

Harnlan was one of those places nobody ever wanted to visit a few years back. Political troubles with the mainland had once made it a dangerous place to be if you weren't in agreement with the locals. Now, however, it had become a touristy haven. Things had calmed down here, and the warm beaches on the south coast made it a cost-effective alternative to a "real" holiday abroad. Neville wasn't here to holiday, however. He was here to exploit the weak-minded and disaffected. It was well known that a minority of Harnlan youths wished for something more than what the old guard sell-out parliamentarians had given them. Not just given, but forced upon them. Neville knew he could harness this ill and turn it into a following for a new way of thinking, a new way based on the book he so closely worshipped. Some people, sadly, would easily be moulded by his actions. People, however disgruntled by the current line-up dishing out orders, would always follow somebody - it was merely a case of getting their attention. Sadly, Neville was now alone... apart from Sharon. Nevertheless, she would certainly figure in his grand scheme. Thanks to Peter, she now did everything that she was told to do. Neville found this ever so wondrous. His mind could not see any issue with it. His mind could not see anything but the book. Darren would have been the outward face of the new leadership, doing his thing as The Leader. Peter would have been behind the scenes, the grand master, making it all happen. Neville saw himself as the faithful servant. Now, only the servant remained. This did not perturb him too much, though. In fact, if anything it spurred him on in his endeavours. As he drew ever nearer to his intended location, he felt more and more strongly that Peter had purposely done himself in in order to transfer his being into Neville. So strong was Neville's belief in this that, by the time they reached Harnlan, he decided Peter's entity *WAS* inside him for sure, and he was now fundamentally two people. Peter Smith, thusly, would still be the manipulator behind the scenes. Neville, the outward partner of this double act, would continue his role as the deliverer of his master's gospel.

ONE HUNDRED YEARS LATER

The girl could not see what Elder Icon could, but felt Its impending arrival. Everyone was connected here. They each felt what the others felt. Or, at least they had been told that they could. She stretched onto her tiptoes, squinting through the window at the wise old woman.

'Hannah,' a voice whispered behind her. She dropped to her knees and scurried behind a bush. 'It's me, Jonny,' he said from the darkness.

'The fat boy?' the girl replied, relaxing and coming out from her hiding place.

'Look what I have,' he whispered, holding up a pair of binoculars.

'What are they?' she asked, puzzled, as he let her hold them. He looked deep into her green eyes and his big heart melted. He so loved this girl. He was just the fat boy, though.

'Come with me, I'll show you.' He took her hand and they ran away from the brook and to the beach. They were not supposed to come here. 'Look through them.'

'These are forbidden,' she gasped. He encouraged her, and she put them to her eyes and looked across the sea. 'I can see the land over there.' She knew Jonny had gotten closer and she put the binoculars back down. They kissed.

The next day, Hannah wasn't there when Elder Icon commenced studies.

'Where's Hannah?' asked Jonny.

'It is not sensible to ask questions,' Elder Icon told the boy.

He knew there and then that she had been taken away since they parted company last night. What could he do?

9PM NEWS: TONIGHT

'Tonight at 10, Peter Smith will commit suicide live on TV and you, the viewers at home, can vote for which method he uses,' Richard repeats. 'The event has just started broadcasting, and suicide prevention worker Felicity Wood has been invited inside the studio. What part she may now play in the show will no doubt become clear as the next hour unfolds. Felicity's last words before accepting the invite inside the studio were direct and summed up her stance: suicide must not be glamourised in this manner. As the world now watches with intent, and those who choose to call in wait poised by their phones for the lines to open, we ask ourselves should we really be devoting so much attention to one man's chosen exist from life? Neville Jeffries believes Peter will rise again and be proven as the deity he claims to be. Is this reason enough for a man to take his own life? Should we allow anyone to take their own life? Do we even have the right to try and stop them? With the recent legalising of assisted dying, and now this broadcast taking place, all of these questions have become that much trickier to answer.'

THE LIVE SUICIDE

'Now is the time, people of the world, to look deep into my eyes,' Neville reels directly at the camera, 'to reveal why Peter Smith has hidden from public view until now. There is a very good reason for this. You see, it is because *I* am Peter Smith. I have kept away from public view until such a time as I was ready to unleash myself onto all of you - to open myself up to your heart's desires. *I* wrote *I AM DEAD*, and *I* will be committing suicide tonight. Committing suicide, with your help. My friends, my followers; assist me. Wield the utmost power most of you will ever have. End my life, and I will resurrect myself to prove my might.'

'I truly believe I speak for Neville when I plead with you: do not allow this to happen. Here, clearly, is a very depressed and deluded man who thinks the only option in life left to him is to die. We must be the ones to provide help for his sad situation,' Felicity, sitting beside him, goes.

'I'm not your husband, Felicity,' Neville laughs. 'You're a lone voice. The crowd wants to help me, they *WILL* help me, and I will guide them on how to do so. They will follow me. The phone lines are now open, and the options are...'

A cheesy voice playfully announces: 'Call the number, and add: 1 for poison, 2 for hanging, 3 for overdose, 4 for suffocation, 5 for jumping from a great height-' the list goes on.

'The best part about dying is not having to get out of bed the following morning,' Neville laughs, winking at the camera.

CUT TO COMMERCIALS

Felicity looked at Neville as his makeup was touched up during the adverts.

'Why, Neville? Truly, why?' she begged him, desperate to save a life from an awful undignified end.

The Space is a portal which will allow me to skip in between all the various alternate realities in the multiverse,' was his response.

'Neville, it's just a book. It's all make-believe.'

'No, no, no. It's real. I have faith in its reality. I have seen things. Peter has passed his link to The Space onto me. I am now the final link between The Great Collective and The Space.'

'What is The Great Collective?'

'I don't know, but I will soon find out. I will come back and tell you. So many things left unexplained,' he lamented, taking from his pocket Peter's old notepad marked *THE MUSEUM CLUB MURDERS*.

'Neville,' she put her hand on his as the makeup man finished and tried to start on her, 'this isn't right. You're a very ill man. I can help you.'

He looked down at her hand. 'You can help me by voting. More funds for printing copies of the book, you see.' He sniffed, clearing his throat. A tear rolled down his cheek and he tried to choke them back. 'There's no escape now,' he continued, 'this is my fate.'

'And we're back in three, two...' the director declares.

'The lines are buzzing,' Neville beams, the makeup hiding the terror Felicity can now sense from him. 'Let's now go out on the streets and see what you're all saying about my impending suicide...'

'Can do what he wants, can't he!' one woman standing on a street calls out into the microphone. 'Don't let that stuck up cow Felicity put a downer on it, I reckon. Power to the people!'

'Neville *IS* the people,' the man beside her explains, 'he speaks for the common hard-working man like me. We all want to escape our hard lives once in a while.'

'This will be a permanent escape,' the reporter explains.

'It's legal now, isn't it? Nothing you can do about it, then. They've made it legal, like gays marrying, so we can't stop that either.'

'Are you equating gay marriage to a live televised suicide?' the reporter asks for confirmation.

'Hey, don't go trying to get some kind of scandal out of me, mate.'

Another man rushes up to the gathering. 'This is tragic. Is this how low we've sunk as a species? Shame on you, humanity,' he calls out.

'We're causing quite a stir, Felicity, and it looks like popularity polls are placing me ahead of you,' Neville rolls with laughter as he turns to a screen displaying a graph. 78% are in favour of him, 22% for her.

'I'm not a part of this.' She suddenly realises how she's been drawn in. She was *ASSISTING* as much as anyone else. Getting up to leave, she looks down at Neville. 'This is your last chance. Come with me now.'

'I can't. I signed a contract.' Neville looks directly into the camera again, reading from the auto-cue as Felicity storms off: 'Suicide prevention has let me down, people. I guess even those with the biggest front quit in the end.'

Felicity fled down a corridor in the studio and came to a door at the end of it. She opened it, stepping inside. It was just a small room, various devices for committing suicide kept in storage in it. A bottle of pills, a length of rope - you name it. She picked the rope up, the now-dulling image of her husband's nude lifeless body dangling out of the attic in her mind. She never thought the horrific scene would become so dull and so stale in her recollection. Forever she would be plagued by it, but time and her busy life had somewhat ebbed its former power. Long had she contemplated suicide herself, and now Reaping Icon appeared beside her.

'No,' he said, which was odd for him. 'This is not for you, Felicity. *YOU* are not to blame for anything. Sometimes people just can't see a way forward. Look, that's all you need to do - look.'

She looked up, and he'd gone.

Neville, the biggest grin that he'd ever managed to force on his face, checked his watch. Time was nearing. He couldn't quite believe what was going on - a situation he himself had created. There was no getting out of it, he'd signed a contract and *HAD* to fulfil its requirements. Nothing was to break the contract. It was as tight as a crab's arse. Nevertheless, Neville felt sure his death would merely allow him to shed his corporeal existence and gain access to the waiting room where Peter had apparently ended up. There was always the element of doubt, however, but it was all too late for that now. Silly Neville.

THE MUSEUM CLUB MURDERS

'Oh really Sally, you cannot be serious! Louis Sellers dead?' usurped the less aged than usual Mother, intermittently sipping at her tea. Her rotund frame flummoxed in forlorn hysteria. She was less aged for good reason - this occurred in the past. I was but a teen, full of glorious youth and vibrant vitality.

'Murdered,' confirmed the equally figurative Aunt Sally, nibbling at her digestive. Mother eyed cautiously the biscuit's congregating crumbs on the flower-patterned carpet.

The living room was dank, the poor lighting concealing much of the tobacco-stained walls. The two ladies, dressed in the same grey cardigan-based garb, sat across from each other in the centre of the room in identical armchairs. A small table separated the women, upon which sat a plethora of biscuits and other nibbles. This was Aunt Sally's downstairs flat, and she was proud of her "homely" abode.

'But when, dear sister?' asked the bemused Mother from her dusty throne.

'Early this morning. Barbara Davies found him in his office,' Aunt Sally went on, 'battered about the head and strangled, I hear. Poor chap, his blood was smeared up the walls apparently.' Aunt Sally leant forward, clearing her throat. 'Also, his penis was out.'

'I see,' replied a cynical Mother, scratching her flocculent chin.

I sat back in my chair. 'How did YOU get to know the sordid details, Aunt Sally?' I asked, gazing through the window indifferently. My chair, purposely positioned some distance from my aunt and her sister, Mother, swivelled around ever so slowly. I turned to face the two gabbling gobblers.

'Oh well, I'm the Museum Caretaker aren't I? When the Chairman is found murdered in his office, I'm bound to be one of the first to be informed,' she revealed, taking obvious delight in the importance she felt she held at the museum. Not yet acquainted with the place myself, I was hitherto unsure of her position. She may well have been a big noise there, though I doubted it. I was right to doubt, too.

'Hmm,' I muttered under my breath as I searched my vast vocabulary for a reply. I studied Mother's wiry hair laboriously, though she did not notice my scrutiny. Her mind was obviously elsewhere. Struggling to fight the beginnings of early dementia, perchance?

'Seems to me like Barbara Davies most probably phoned you up to tell you all the gory details,' Mother exclaimed.

'Well naturally, she and I have been friends for many years now. She tells me everything, and I mean everything!' Aunt Sally gloated.

'Did she ever mention her illicit affair with Louis Sellers, Aunt Sally?' I asked bluntly. 'After all, his penis WAS out.'

Mother's jaw dropped, possibly a shock reaction to my mention of the male member.

'Indeed not! Barbara is far too young for Louis Sellers, how could you think of such a thing?' asked Aunt Sally unhesitatingly. 'Besides, what has his penis got to do with Barbara Davies?'

'Just trying to establish a motive. Perhaps Barbara Davies didn't just find Louis Sellers, perhaps she did him in in the first place.' I remained calm and collected as I looked upon the two ladies, now hanging on my every word.

'Oh no, she couldn't possibly have done that to him, he was in a terrible mess,' she replied. 'I assume the penis was mutilated.'

'Assumptions can be presumptuous. Besides, that's what Barbara told you. Perhaps it was just a pill in his whiskey that finished him off?' I continued, deliciously indulging in speculation. Whilst Aunt Sally growled with disdain at the sheer mention of this, Mother tapped at her thin lips.

'Now steady on, Sally,' she came in, 'remember when Barbara Davies borrowed that set of Sheffield steel spoons off me?' she asked with a grin, eagerly awaiting a response.

'What about them?'

'Well, I have yet to have them back from her, and the dinner party, to which I was not invited, occurred over two months ago. Solve that one for me!' exclaimed Mother, quickly coming round to the idea that Barbara Davies was a brutal murderer.

'Let me remind you that there is quite some difference between forgetting to return some borrowed spoons, and garrotting and battering to death a fully-grown man,' explained Aunt Sally, finding herself as Barbara Davies' defence in the debate. 'No, no,' she continued, 'Barbara Davies is neither capable of having an affair with, nor murdering, a man.'

'And, Barbara Davies is not married, is she?'

'Well, what of it?'

'So if it wasn't Barbara Davies, then who was it?' asked Mother, wishing to settle the matter once and for all.

'How should I know, I'm not a detective,' blasted a defensive Aunt Sally, becoming quite upset at the whole affair. Why she was defending Barbara Davies was anyone's guess.

'No you're not a detective, but I know a man who is,' I exclaimed, rising from my seat aberrantly, my stiff collar causing only minor discomfort. 'I shall go and see him at once.'

'Show some deference dear boy, Aunt Sally has yet to finish her tea and biscuits,' ejaculated Mother abrasively.

'Oh of course, please forgive my manners.' I sat back down, taking a sip from the cup of tea designated for my consumption.

'You seen this?' roared Inspector Hastings, waving a letter about his sergeant's face.

'No, Sir,' replied Sergeant Noose respectfully. The inspector thrust the letter into the hands of the unsuspecting, and rather tired, sergeant. Yes, here was Noose the young man, a full head of hair to his name and, as yet, relatively uncontaminated from my impending barrage into his life.

'You take a look at that. Raucous, me? Rubbish!' exclaimed Hastings.

'Indeed, Sir,' Noose, somewhat indifferent, replied whilst reading the letter.

'Rubbish! Somebody complaining about me? *ME*? Huh, I thought the police were supposed to be respected. If I exert respect to people, even criminals, you'd think they'd respect me back. Wouldn't you, Sergeant?' Noose, attempting to focus his mind on reading the letter, nodded at his inspector, but this wasn't enough. Hastings began pumping his arms in the air, grasping at the ever thinning oxygen above his scalp. 'You hear me, Noose?'

'Yes Sir, if you exerted respect you would get respected back,' exclaimed Noose right back.

'Exactly, Sergeant. So why do we get fools like this wishing to make formal complaints?' raged Hastings, seemingly bemused by the whole episode. He seemed a bit overwhelmed with disappointment, rather than shame, and made a number of scowling expressions.

'A mystery only a detective inspector can unravel, Sir.' Noose passed the letter back to his superior. He scratched the side of his head. 'Anything else, Sir? he asked woefully.

'Ah yes, Sergeant. This dead bloke, murdered,' Hastings blabbed bluntly.

'Yes?' asked Noose, expecting a list of instructions.

'Yes, annoying isn't it?' Hastings remarked. 'It seems we've made a blunder.'

'*WE*, Sir?'

'Yes, we. As in you and me, not as in urinating. You were there, Sergeant, and I expect you to take fifty percent of the blame.'

'I don't think the press will accept that I caused fifty percent of this blunder you speak of, as they always seem to blame you one hundred percent when slip-ups occur,' regaled Noose.

'Yes, well... I would hope that your loyalty to your superior officer would imply that you help him out in times of need.'

'You mean, take half the rap?'

'So to speak, yes. Oh for goodness sake Henry, it's not a matter of life or death. It wouldn't kill you, would it?' The inspector rose to his feet, shuffling ever so slightly forward.

'Taking in mind that if this blunder is what I think it is, then it *MAY* in fact be, ironically, a matter of life and death.'

'Oh come now, Sergeant,' chuckled Hastings, attempting to make light of the situation by lightly tapping Noose on the shoulder with his fist.

'Sir, you destroyed the murder weapon used to kill Louis Sellers, and any DNA or fingerprints that may have been on it!'

'Well if you take the whole thing out of context, Henry, I grant you it does sound quite serious, but honestly! Anyway, how was I to know that the wood wasn't for the fire?'

'Some might question why you wished to start the fire at a murder scene in the first place,' Noose pointed out.

'It is winter, *SERGEANT*.' Hastings moved over to the fish tank in his office and tapped at the glass. 'Besides, the murderer was wearing gloves, so no fingerprints would have shown up anywhere.'

'And how do we know that, Sir?' asked the lucid Noose.

'Well there are no fingerprints on Sellers' neck, are there!' exclaimed Hastings. 'Now Sergeant, Noose... Henry... when the, erm, Chief Superintendent asks whether or not we have found a murder weapon, you know what you'll have to say don't you…'

'That you burnt it?'

'*NO* Sergeant, no, you must tell her that… that we haven't yet found one.' The inspector's hands clenched as he stared at the fish tank.

'I can't do that Sir, besides, Lucy saw the murder weapon too. She saw you throw it on the fire.'

'Damn, I'd forgotten about that work experience girl.' Hastings' hands relaxed stoically. 'Well, there's nothing else for it - we'll have to solve the case before the superintendent gets back from her trip.'

'That gives you until tomorrow evening, Sir,' Noose quickly pointed out.

'Correction, that gives *US* until tomorrow evening, Sergeant.'

Having eavesdropped on the entire conversation from just the other side of the door, I was keener than ever to ensure this case had a professional dealing with it: me.

'And you say you saw Barbara Davies arrive at about half seven in the morning? Is that her usual routine?' I asked the man, as he stood at his door. His bushy eyebrows could have done with a trim… and the hair shooting out of his ears. In fact, he looked like an unkempt dog. I, an expectant cat just out of reach of this chained beast, toyed and jostled my way to extracting what I wanted from him.

'Yeah, that's right. Only, there is something odd,' the man told me hesitantly.

'Please, go on,' I encouraged seductively.

'Who are you anyway?' he demanded, bolting angrily. 'You're certainly not from the police, that's for sure.'

'How do you know that?' I asked, ever the seeker of other people's business.

'Well early this morning when the cops were here, my wife went across there to the museum.' He pointed across the street at the tall grey building, as I took in the surprise discovery that this shaggy thin thing had a wife. 'Spoke to an inspector, said she had some information he might find useful. He told her that he didn't need her help.' He rubbed over his stubble with one hand, the other hand plunged deep into his pocket.

'Did he? Well, you can tell me. I'm what you might call a *PRIVATE* investigator.'

'You look like a nosy bugger off the street to me. There's been loads of people buzzin' about the museum all day.' The man stepped further inside his house, taking hold of the door.

'Please can you just tell me what you know. If the police won't listen then I might be the only person who will. You do want to see a murderer brought to justice, don't you?'

'Well of course I do,' the man, glare-eyed, spoke back.

'Good, glad to hear you champion justice, Sir,' I replied, slowly but surely weaning the information off this idiot.

'Well alright then,' he relented, seeing that I was at no present time going to give up. 'You see, Barbara Davies always comes at half seven every morning, my wife gets up at that time and sees her - but never at night. Last night, though, and this is very odd, Barbara Davies turned up at the museum in a different car. We didn't recognise it.'

'And what time was this?' I pushed.

'Well late, must have been after two o'clock. My wife and I were in bed, but when we heard a car across the street, my wife understandably got out of bed to have a look. She saw Barbara Davies get out of the car and go into the museum. Soon enough Barbara came out again, running, and sped off in the car. I heard the screech of the vehicle myself.'

'Is your wife sure it was Barbara Davies?'

'Positive, she has brilliant eyesight you know.'

'I'm quite sure she has.' I looked again at his awful face. Then again, was mine much better? 'Is your wife in now?' I asked, wishing to question her myself before any police could.

'No, she's still at work.'

'I see. Well, thank you.' I turned to leave, but spun around to face him again almost immediately. 'Is your wife sure it was a different car Barbara Davies was driving?' I pushed and pushed, the information suddenly having dawned on him.

'Yes, as I say, her eyesight is second to none. She noticed I was going bald long before I, or anyone else, did!'

'Thank you.' The door was closed on me, and I turned and walked back down the driveway. I stopped at the gate and looked up at the old museum building across the street. A glance up at the window behind me where the man's wife would have seen Barbara Davies in the early hours of the morning served to stir up my suspicions even further. I mounted my bicycle and rode away.

The following interplay, though I was not present during its occurrence, *DID* occur. I know it did, and you are in no position to question me:

'Now, we're off to see Barbara Davies again. Maybe she can give us a little more information on the Museum Club Committee. You know, Sergeant, I think this case will be wrapped up long before the superintendent shows up. We have four suspects, shouldn't take too long to whittle them down to one.' Inspector Hastings opened the car door and stepped in. Sergeant Noose followed.

'Five, Sir,' Noose corrected.

'What?' asked the inspector, trying to put his seatbelt on.

'Five suspects, Sir, I count five. Barbara Davies is also a suspect,' Noose pointed out.

'Oh don't be ridiculous man, she could never have done such a thing to that man.'

'Why not? Men do that sort of thing to women all the time. Why not the other way around, occasionally?' Noose put the key in the ignition and started the car up. They slowly pulled out of the police station car park and on to the main road. 'We must keep an open mind, Sir.'

'Yes you're right, again. It would seem you're not completely stupid after all, Sergeant.'

'Your belief in me positively lifts my spirits, Inspector,' Noose replied swiftly.

'I am convinced that Barbara Davies is the killer,' I clacked with a stolid tongue.

'You can't go jumping to conclusions just like that, Peter. Besides, you've never even met Barbara Davies so how do you know what she is like, what she is capable of?' Mother fired back, enjoying the barter she shared with me.

'The fact that I don't know Barbara Davies is something soon to be rectified, Mother,' I shot back with a pistol of defiance.

'Go on then, run along. Aunt Sally told you where she lives. Go and enjoy your amateur detective work. I'll just sit here and eat my beans on toast alone again.' I rose from my seat and left the kitchen. Why she couldn't have waited for Father to return home from work, or Stuart from school, was anybody's guess. Already, it seemed, she and I were developing this beguiling bond. 'You really should find yourself a job, boy,' she shouted after me, 'that way, at least, I may stand at least a slim chance of getting some keep from you.'

The car pulled up outside Barbara Davies' house. Noose turned the ignition off and, ushered by his superior, stepped out of the car and locked the doors. The two made their way to the front door, little noticing the twitching net-curtain in the front downstairs window. Before they had a chance to knock on the door, it had been opened. A tall, well-built woman in her early thirties presented herself in the doorway. She seemed to stand much taller than the two men, even though Inspector Hastings was a giant of a man. Despite the apparent height difference, her eyes seemed to meet Sergeant Noose's quite comfortably. Hastings coughed in discomfort as he found his immediate line of sight filled with the rather hefty bust of this fine woman.

'Hello again, Miss Davies,' Hastings spoke, after a moment of hesitation. 'Good afternoon,' he added.

'Please Inspector, I wish to be alone,' she said abrasively, her eyes tearful.

'I know today has been a shock for you Miss Davies, but could we please come in? We have some questions we wish to ask. Besides, technically you should have accompanied us down to the station this morning for questioning.'

'Somebody should be with you,' Noose added, looking up at her face. He feared for his sanity should he allow her ample bosom to blossom in his mind. He ignored it, and with good reason - things had not been simple for him at home of late. I knew all about that.

'I'm fine, honestly. I've answered all of your questions, Inspector - what more could you want from me?'

Hastings, vast breasts ensconcing him, cleared his throat in trepidation.

'He wants to know why you killed Louis Sellers!' I exclaimed, riding up the path on my bicycle.

'Peter!' Noose sighed, turning to look at me, the amateur sleuth, nearing.

'Inspector Hastings, Sergeant Noose! How are you two keeping?' I asked joyfully.

'How could you even think I'd killed Louis? I'd never harm anyone,' Barbara cried out after a prolonged preparation.

'A rather slow, measured response,' I mused. 'I have every right to accuse you, knowing what I do.'

'What are you on about, Peter? What do you know?' Hastings yelled.

'So you want my help do you, Hastings? That's a bit out of character. When I offered my services on the work experience programme, you sent me packing.'

'Just tell us what you know, Peter,' Noose intervened in his usual calm and collected cadence. He was a splendid man, looking upon me with patience and respect.

'Wait a moment,' Hastings interrupted, realising that all of this was happening in the front garden. 'Do you mind if we come in, Miss Davies, you don't want your neighbours knowing all of your business now, do you?'

Barbara stood aside and we three men stepped into the house. Noose looked up and smiled at Barbara as he passed, realising just how short he was compared to her. I kept my head down and turned to one side until the front door was closed. The four of us congregated in the living room, where I helped myself to a seat.

'Why don't you sit down whilst you accuse me of murder!' Barbara bawled at me.

'Thank you, I will.' I looked about the room, wondering which of the myriad of boxes and drawers currently housed Mother's Sheffield steel spoons.

'Come on Peter, what's this all about?' asked Hastings patronisingly, cautious as to how to approach a man he saw as potentially mentally unstable. There was no potential about it... I was completely fucked up.

'I believe that you, Barbara, killed Louis Sellers,' I said bluntly, pointing at the beast of a wench. I closed one eye, looking up at my fingertip. It appeared to be touching one of Barbara's sheathed nipples.

'As I've just told you, and will tell you again, I did not kill him. Why on earth won't you listen?'

'I won't listen because I have some evidence, that I have

gathered myself, which incriminates you.' Again I pointed at her, one eye closed.

'Go on then, enlighten us,' Hastings urged, growing restless with anticipation.

'Just over an hour ago I had a chat with somebody, who shall remain nameless at present.' Noose rolled his eyes and folded his arms. I continued: 'This person, who is remaining nameless of course, told me that his wife witnessed you driving away from the museum in the early hours of the morning. You were driving erratically, and not in your own car. Inspector Hastings, at what time was Louis Sellers murdered?' I asked. Barbara remained silent, taking in what I was telling her.

'Between two and four o'clock, why?'

'It was after two that the witness saw Barbara drive away.'

'Alright, alright, I was there,' she blurted out, forcing out a tear. 'Is that what you wanted to here?'

'It'll do for a start, yes.' Hastings turned in shock to face her, taking charge of the situation. 'Come on, what's all this about?' he pushed further.

'Okay, I was there. Half two in the morning.' She sat down on the sofa and put her arms on her lap.

'So you did do it!' I declared, hardly able to believe I may have stumbled over the solution to the slaughter.

'No, I did not. You see, Louis phoned me up at about two in the morning. He, erm, he told me he was in some trouble. He wanted me to come and help him at once.' She stared at the floor, taking up no eye contact with any of us in the room.

'What sort of trouble?' asked Noose.

'He didn't say, but I could take a wild guess.'

'Go on...' urged Noose, catching a whiff of the finishing post.

'Oh, I can't say. I may be wrong, I wouldn't like to make anyone a suspect.'

'No, go on,' Noose continued.

'Well, you see… Money has been going missing - large amounts. Louis suspected the treasurer, James Harrington, had something to do with it.'

'Did he now?' I added, sceptical, turning away to glance out of the window.

'Yes. In fact, the two came to blows a few nights back at one of the committee meetings. The others will vouch for that.'

'I bet they will.'

'Quiet Peter, we may be on to something here,' Noose came in, giving me an ambiguous stare. 'Why didn't you tell us all this before, Miss Davies?'

'I, I thought you might suspect me. If I'd have contacted the police in the middle of the night you'd have suspected me straight away, wondering why I was at the museum at such a time.'

'You could have told us the truth, saved us all this bother,' Hastings sighed, checking his watch.

'The door was open. Louis was just lying there, dead. I panicked. It was a terrible mess. I didn't know what to do, so I just got back in my car and drove away. I haven't even slept yet.'

'In somebody else's car!' I interrupted, gleeful that she had slipped up in her lies.

'No, I was in my own car. Your witness must be mistaken.'

I now glanced at my watch, and back at Barbara. I was confused, and made no attempt to hide the fact. 'So my witness gets everything else right, apart from the car? The time, the erratic driving?' I stood up and stepped towards Barbara, standing shoulder to shoulder with Noose and turning to look him in the eye. 'Everything but the car,' I mumbled under my breath.

'I can't explain. Your witness must be mistaken. I live alone, I've only got one car.'

'Yes, my witness must be mistaken,' I quickly relented. 'I apologise for accusing you of murder, Miss Davies.' I left the living room and idled in the hall.

'Sergeant, we'll have to check with the phone company that a call was made,' Hastings informed Noose.

'Yes, Sir.'

'Miss Davies, you really should have told us earlier. All of this could have been avoided,' Hastings pointed out.

'I'm sorry Inspector, I panicked. I didn't kill Louis. I've seen what prisons are like, why would I want to end up in one by killing somebody?' Barbara gave a forced laugh as she looked at the two men still in the room, before fixing her stare once more on the floor.

I, having been listening from the hallway, turned to look at Barbara's telephone. Next to it on the table was a small book with a brown cover. I quietly opened it, and peeked inside. It contained telephone numbers, all names listed alphabetically by surname. I turned immediately to the section for surnames beginning with 'S'. I could see no listing for Louis Sellers. I quickly replaced the book in its original position and moved back into the living room.

'We will have to question you further, but that can wait. The important thing is for you to get some rest now, Miss Davies,' Noose told her softly.

'Why did Louis phone you, Miss Davies?' I suddenly asked, politely enough though.

'I, I don't know. We are, we were, close friends. I've been a committee member for six years, we know each other well.'

'I see. Well, I think it's time I was going,' I announced, and once again I headed out of the room.

'Yes, we must be going now too. If there is anything else you can tell us about James Harrington, now would be a good time,' Hastings declared.

'That's all I know. You'll have to ask him if you want to know anything else Inspector, I'm sorry.'

'Okay. Right, I want a word with him,' Hastings announced, marching after me.

'Thank you Miss Davies, but please be honest with us in future, won't you. Shock or not,' Noose told her, before following his superior out of the room.

Barbara closed the door behind them. I mounted my bicycle and began to ride down the path.

'Hey, stop there right now, you,' Hastings called out to me.

'Yes, Inspector?' I called back drolly.

'You think she did it, don't you?'

'Answer me this, Inspector,' I slid coyly, 'if she was such a good pal to Louis Sellers, how come he's not even in her personal phone book?'

'How do you know that?'

'I had a look when I was in the hall.'

'He may have a point, Sir,' Noose added.

'Well, for the time being I think we should pay this James Harrington a visit. Barbara Davies can wait. She's not going anywhere.'

Hastings and Noose made their way past me and headed for the car. I pushed my bicycle to the nearest lamppost and proceeded to chain it up. Without warning I opened the back door of Noose's saloon and jumped in.

'What on earth do you think you're doing?' Hastings roared at me from the front passenger seat.

'Well I've been handy up to now, haven't I? You might need my help at this Harrington chap's house.' Before waiting for a reply, I put my belt on. 'What are we waiting for, you two? Don't you know where he lives or something?'

'Just step on it Henry, we'd have to lock him up to get him off our backs.'

'So you do know the way?' I joked.

'We have the addresses of all the museum committee members,' Noose explained.

'Bizarre, isn't it, the world of the criminal mind,' I uttered from the back seat.

'Keep your mouth shut, you're in the real world of detection now you know,' Hastings growled. I eyed up a comic book sitting on the seat next to me and turned to look at the back of their heads once again.

'We certainly are in the real world, Inspector. This is what life is all about.' I sat back and relaxed my shoulders.

The car crept along the curb towards James Harrington's house, wheezing like an old small dog might if the owner was walking it too much. It came to a stop as Hastings motioned towards the house with his finger. I was the first out of the car, ever eager to put my growing detective skills to good use. The house, seemingly split up into two flats, appeared empty. Curtains were drawn downstairs, and hung precariously off the rails upstairs.

'Looks empty, Sir,' Noose remarked, following his superior up the path.

'I can see that,' Hastings shot back.

I allowed the two to pass me, wishing instead to trail behind to see Noose in action. Noose tried the two bells on the door - no reply. The men were not even sure the bells were working, as no pleasant jingle followed the pressing of them. Without warning, the next door neighbour's door flew open. An elderly gentleman wobbled out.

'I saw you come up the path, who are you?' he asked in a high-pitched voice.

'Good evening, we're the police. I'm Inspector-' Hastings began, but was interrupted by the man.

'Eh? You'll 'ave to speak up, I'm deaf.'

'We're looking for Mr Harrington - James Harrington,' Noose told the man, repeating the same high-pitched voice the man had used. Hastings took out his wallet to show the man his identification.

"Aven't seen 'im. Lives there on 'is own, you know. Odd chap. One of them 'omosexuals most likely. You rentin' the downstairs or something?'

'We're the police, Sir,' Noose told him, 'we want to have a word with Mr Harrington.'

'Caught him gettin' up to mischief, eh? Might be in there. Then again, he might not. Never goes anywhere, except that museum. I'm told someone's been murdered, is it true? Is that what this is about, eh? Harrington's done it, 'asn't he?'

'We don't know that, not yet anyway,' Noose tried to explain, hoping to avoid neighbourhood gossip.

'Look, have you seen any sign of anyone here recently?' asked Hastings, his patience dwindling fast.

'Come again?'

'Has anyone been here recently?' Hastings yelled down the man's ear.

'Now come to think of it, yes. A woman, that I'm sure of.'

'What did this woman look like?' I suddenly asked the man, stepping closer to him.

'Couldn't tell you, it was in the night, last night I think. Just got my new glasses today as well. Sat on the last pair.'

I dropped back once again, deep in thought. This must have been Barbara.

'Well, was she tall, short, fat, thin?' Noose asked, continuing the doorstep interrogation.

'Honestly couldn't tell you, it was dark.'

'So how do you know it was a woman then?' asked Noose, becoming ever intrigued himself.

'Massive honkers, lots of hair.'

'You could spot her *HONKERS* and hair, yet you couldn't tell whether she was fat or thin?' I sighed in exasperation.

'What about your wife, Sir? Maybe she saw something,' Hastings suggested.

'Well if she did she didn't tell me, she's been dead five years. I live alone.'

'Alone! Everybody lives alone!' Hastings grunted, flinging his arms into the air in frustration.

'This is pointless, Sir, we're getting nowhere with this,' Noose whispered to Hastings, making sure the neighbour could not hear him.

'I think we should go and take a look in his flat,' I suggested, stepping up to the door to inspect the lock.

'If he won't come to the door, we'll have to get a warrant to enter,' Hastings explained, thoroughly dismayed with the situation.

'What if he *CAN'T* come to the door?' I suggested, brandishing a small toffee hammer from one of my many pockets and smashing a small pane of glass in the front door.

'What the hell do you think you're doing?' yelled a shocked Hastings, disinterested with the fact that the volume of his voice could now stir even the deafest person in the neighbourhood.

'I saw nothing,' chuckled the neighbour, before adjusting his new spectacles in an attempt to gain a clearer view of the action.

'They always have one of these locks you can open from the inside without a key, don't they Inspector. Catches,' I exclaimed, turning to smile at my audience as I reached through the broken window.

'Shall I read him his rights, Sir?' Noose asked calmly.

'No, he may be on to something. His instincts might pay off,' Hastings replied, holding on to Noose as he stepped in front of me and inside. Noose and I followed. Only today's post blocked the door, allowing our inquisitive bodies to progress unhindered up the stairs.

'Bottom flat looks empty, alright,' Noose observed.

The flat door at the top of the stairs was ajar. We pushed it open and stepped inside. The smell of stale cigarettes hit all three of our noses, as too did another smell - a smell rather staler than cigarettes. Noose hastily headed for the living room. A grisly sight awaited him. He froze, clutching his jaw. Hastings pushed past him through the door, before recoiling in horror. The two men, speechless, made the way clear for me. I stood at the door frame, motionless, staring at the mutilated corpse in front of me - the penis the main focus of the slicing and dicing. It had been split in two.

'I'll take a wild stab in the dark,' I exclaimed, 'that is James Harrington.'

'Looks like he tore the curtains down in the struggle,' Noose surmised, sitting on the edge of the office chair.

'I was speechless... me! Never before in my career have my eyes met such a ferocious sight. It was even worse than Louis Sellers,' Hastings blurted out, staring at his fish tank. 'I only hope he was dead when the sick bastard did that to his cock.'

'But ultimately committed by the same person,' I confidently exclaimed.

'Well Harrington was a lot younger than Sellers, he'd have put up much more of a fight. Terrible!' Noose replied.

'There's one sick bastard out there,' Hastings gasped, deep in reflection of the horrors that had met his eyes. I wasn't really that bothered. It intrigued me more than horrified.

'Do you know what makes both of these murders so bizarre?' I asked, anticipating no particular response.

'Both had their penises mutilated?' Noose sighed.

'No signs of forced entry. In both cases, Louis Sellers and James Harrington knew their murderer. They let their murderer in - must have done.'

'No forced entry at the museum! There are only two people who have keys to the museum, the curator and Louis Sellers, and the curator has an alibi that no jury would question!' Noose added.

'And Aunt Sally the caretaker,' I added.

'Well she's not exactly a caretaker, more of a cleaner. She has no key, the curator locks up apparently - or Louis Sellers, if he ever stayed late,' Noose explained to me. I pondering upon Aunt Sally's response had she heard her coveted position on the museum staff being belittled in this manner.

'I think we should interview more committee members, get a real picture of what goes on,' I trundled on. 'We've got four committee members left now.'

'Don't get too comfortable Peter, you're not a police officer. Besides, I should arrest you for breaking that window,' Hastings went on.

'But you're not going to, are you?' I chuckled confidently.

'Look Peter, I'm running this investigation, not you. If you want to help then you take orders from me, not the other way around, understand?'

'Yes, Boss,' I declared sarcastically, standing to attention and saluting. Noose raised an eyebrow as I sat back in my chair. Hastings seemed to be doing well at humouring me, greeting my actions with mild confusion.

'I have a vague recollection that something like this has happened before,' Hastings explained, attempting to rack his brains. 'Yes, before I got here. I remember reading some file or other on the museum. I transferred to this station seven years ago, so it was before that. Check it out, could lead to something.'

'Right,' Noose acknowledged, before rising to his feet.

'And you go with him too, Peter, I can't bear to look at your face any longer. I'm depressed enough as it is.' Hastings flopped into the back of his chair and spun around to face the window. I stood up to follow Noose out of the room.

'Lovely office,' I exclaimed, 'always wanted a desk myself, but Mother said we can't fit it anywhere.' With this said I followed Noose out, leaving Hastings to gather his thoughts.

The early morning sun broke through the blinds of the office window, piercing Hastings' grey skin. He woke up with a start, quickly realising he had fallen asleep soon after Noose and I had left. It was now morning, and there was no sign of either of us. The morning paper sat on his desk. He straightened his back and rubbed at his side as the full realisation of the pain in his back took force. He picked the paper up and read the headline on the front cover. His jaw dropped. Suddenly Noose and I appeared from behind him. Noose sat down and sipped at a mug of coffee. I fiddled with the blinds as I glanced outside.

'This is it. This is what I remember,' Hastings yelled.

'Of course it is,' I fired back. 'Only problem is, we had to read it in a newspaper to find out. We were up all night searching through files, didn't come across anything. Then, we read the morning paper!'

'Well why didn't you wake me up when it arrived?' Hastings demanded, rising from his chair with a jerk.

'We thought we'd let you have a little rest before you had to face the media again,' Noose explained.

'What?'

'They're after you this time, you know. One slip-up on top of another with you, isn't it?' I snorted.

'Damn! And you couldn't find anything in the files? We're only a small station!' Hastings exclaimed. 'Wait a second,' he gulped, eyeing up a stack of papers on his desk. A closer inspection revealed a brown folder marked Watkins Case Files. 'This is it. On my desk all the time.'

Noose threw himself into the back of a chair and dropped his arms either side of it.

'It appears I've made another slip-up, doesn't it?!' Hastings laughed.

I picked up the newspaper and read out the headline: 'Sellers' butchered by copycat killer.'

'Good job that went to print before they caught wind of James Harrington,' replied Noose.

Hastings opened the Watkins Case Files and glanced through the pages.

'Yes, ten years ago. I remember now, he killed a member of the Museum Club whilst trying to mug him. Louis Sellers and James Harrington testified against him at the trial, said they'd seen the whole thing. It's a wonder the media didn't pick up on all of this sooner, they're desperate to see me fail.' Hastings dropped the files onto his desk. 'For goodness sake,' he growled through gritted teeth.

'Watkins is our man,' I blurted out, clutching the paper.

'You've quickly changed your tune haven't you! What happened to your Barbara Davies theory?' Noose asked sarcastically.

'We have a motive here!'

'Why don't you take a look in the files,' Hastings suggested, 'what the paper fails to reveal is that Watkins is dead,' he pointed out, speed-reading.

'What?'

'Died a couple of months back, in prison.'

'I see,' I replied, full of disappointment.

'I'll tell you something else the papers also fail to reveal, and that is that Watkins has a sister. She happens to live across the road from the museum.' The penny dropped. I beamed with surprise as I looked upon the inspector. 'Why didn't I see it before?' Hastings asked himself.

'Across the road as in the old Victorian house with the messy garden?' I asked in disbelief.

'What used to be the Vicarage.'

'She's my witness.'

'Come again?'

'Yes! Well I never saw her, I saw her husband, and he told me she saw Barbara Davies. Well, it's all making sense now. This sister of Watkins did them both in herself in revenge for putting her brother in prison. She probably made Louis Sellers make the phone call to Barbara Davies to set her up for the murders.'

'But why try and set Barbara Davies up?' Noose pondered.

'I don't know, I suppose anybody who would take suspicion off herself would do.'

'Her name is Jane Edwards. I think we should pull her in for questioning, don't you?' Hastings closed the Watkins Case Files and stood up to leave.

'Her husband told me she was in work when I paid them a visit. What if she's already gone to work today?' I asked from the backseat.

'Then we find out where she works and go there, don't we!' Hastings replied in his usual gruff tone.

'I see.' We stepped out of Noose's car and headed up the path. 'See, look at the garden. Messy isn't it?' I pointed out. 'They could do with hiring me to tidy it up.'

'Is that what you're doing with yourself now you've finished school?' asked Noose.

'Yes, I help the elderly cultivate their land.'

Hastings knocked on the door. A rather petite woman answered it.

'Hello,' she said, recognising Hastings. 'I've been expecting you.'

'You have?' asked Hastings, taken aback at what he thought a confession.

'Please, step in.' She ushered us inside her home.

Her husband was sitting at the kitchen table, and glanced up as he read the morning paper. I helped myself to a seat next to the man in an attempt to see what he was reading.

'Mrs Edwards, where were you in the early hours of yesterday morning, between the hours of-?' Noose began, but was cut off by Jane.

'I was across the road murdering Louis Sellers,' she said calmly, before picking up a mug of coffee. She sipped at it gently. We were astonished at her supposed confession, her husband merely continuing at his reading task. 'Oh yes, that's what you want to hear, isn't it - that I battered and strangled him to death, because my innocent brother was set-up by the man?'

'Mrs Jane Edwards, I arrest you for the murder of Louis Sellers, and James Harrington,' Hastings declared, signalling Noose to take a grip of her arm. Shock filled her face. She turned to look at her husband, who didn't seem to be taking a blind bit of notice or interest in the action taking place in his kitchen.

'James is dead as well?' she asked, appearing surprised and flustered.

'You have the right to remain silent, but anything you do say may be taken down and given as evidence against you in a court of law,' Noose finished.

'Very professional, Sergeant, I like it,' I chuckled.

The interview room was familiar to me, having been questioned in there myself on many occasions. I was always a suspect in petty crimes in the area, as I was always sticking my nose in to try and solve them. This time, however, I was not allowed in. It was down to Inspector Hastings and Sergeant Noose to question Jane Edwards. Whether or not I believed that her arrest was a little in haste did not matter, for I did not technically have the right to have any direct input into the case. That's why, at this present moment in time, I was sitting in a waiting room usually designated to people waiting to see a family member who had been arrested. A short, gorgeous dark-haired girl opened the door. I knew who she was as we'd been in school together. She was Lucy Davies - no relation to Barbara Davies, of course. She eyed me over with suspicion, as if she somehow suspected me of being some riff-raff off the streets waiting to see my trouble-making pal. She knew who I was, though. Everyone in school knew who I was. And, everyone in school disliked me. She was no exception. I also disliked her, intensely, as she had landed the work experience job at the station. But, oh - she was a Goddess to my sight, surrounding me in her splendour. She wore some kind of doctor's uniform, accentuating her amazing freshly-formed breasts, and held a clipboard in one hand.

'I'm Peter,' I told her, full of confidence even though I could see she was stunning. I knew there was no chance between us of anything occurring, and this helped me appear full of myself. 'We were in school together, remember?'

'No,' she replied.

'Lucy Davies, you were in the other classroom down the hallway to mine.'

'That's me.'

'What are you doing here?' I asked quickly, even though I knew the answer.

'I was supposed to come and get you, old Hastings has something he wants to tell you.'

'And he sent you? Where's his dog's body Noose?' I joked, trying to be a bit hip. She smiled half-heartedly at my jest, but was not warming to me. I could feel her cold indifference. I could warm her up very easily, if only she wanted me to. I moved closer to where she stood in the doorway. She moved out of the way, and we headed down the corridor. I walked behind her, lost in the yo-yo of her tight bum cheeks as they politely took it in turns to bob up and down for me - splaying and rippling for my pleasure.

Some time had now passed between Jane Edwards being brought in, and me now walking into Hastings' office. Lucy left me at the door, heading back down the corridor we had just walked up. I felt sure she and I would meet again in the near future. I felt I *HAD* to make a meeting happen.

'Sit down Peter, we have good news,' Hastings announced, sat comfortably at his desk.

'Really?'

'Tell him, Sergeant.'

'Well, it appears Jane Edwards *IS* the murderer,' Noose smirked.

'Does it? What about forensic evidence, blood on her clothes etc? It's all very fast?' I remained standing near the door, unsure as to whether I should sit down or not. This was unusual for me.

'Well, forensics will find something in her house. It's all just a matter of time. Let's hope this is all wrapped up before the superintendent gets back this evening.' Hastings picked up a pen and put it in his pocket. 'You've met Lucy then, have you Peter?' Hastings suddenly asked him.

'Yes, just now,' I replied, a big grin on my face.

'Helping us out around the place. We've all taken to her, you know. She'd make a fine police officer one day.'

'Oh yes?' I chuckled.

'Keep out of her way,' he warned me. I lost my composure in surprise for but a moment, quickly regaining my usual, and purposeful, nonplussed facial expression. 'We don't want you harassing her like you harass us. Got it?'

'Yup.'

'I mean it. Don't pollute her mind with your fanciful mischief. Anyway, what I'm trying to say is that you can go home now, let the professionals sort the serious stuff out. Thanks for the help.' Hastings smiled, taking great satisfaction in dismissing my services and once again taking full control of the situation.

'Okay, fair enough. I'll, I'll leave you to it then. Goodbye.' I headed straight out of the room, shutting the door behind me. I pressed my ear up to the door and listened.

'Well, that was strange. We usually can't shake him off, can we Henry?' Hastings puzzled, pondering why I had left so easily.

'Ah yes, this is the one,' the police officer spoke, fishing out a chain of keys from his trouser pocket.

'A very old-fashioned police station this, isn't it?' I remarked as I looked upon the officer fiddling with the lock of the door.

'Hasn't been renovated since I've been here, and I've been here twenty years.'

The door unlocked, and I was ushered inside.

'Thank you very much, I won't be long.' I stepped inside, keeping my eyes off Jane Edwards.

'I hope you're not long Peter, don't want a noose around my neck!' he laughed.

'What are you going to pin on me now, hey?' Jane asked, perched uncomfortably on the edge of the hard mattress.

'I don't want to pin anything on you, I just want the truth,' I replied, making eye contact with her.

'I've told the other two the truth, go and ask them,' was her defiant answer.

'I'd much rather ask you. Besides, they won't tell me anything. I'd rather hear it from the horse's mouth.'

'As I've told them, I did *NOT* kill Sellers and Harrington. Why would I? I despised my brother.'

'You despised your own brother?'

'Please, don't think I'm callous, he was an awful man. Kept pleading his innocence publicly, became obsessed with claiming he had been set up by Sellers and Harrington, when all the while he kept telling me he had done it! Wanted to clear his name! He was as guilty as Cain was for killing Abel.'

'Why did he admit to you that he'd done it if he was trying to clear his name?' I asked, intrigued, coming to sit next to her.

'He was a sick man, mentally. He got a thrill out of twisting people, manipulating them. He could have you believing his every word at the drop of a hat, but I didn't fall for it. Oh, he was obsessed with telling people how he'd been framed by the museum committee. Kept spouting rubbish about them hiding something - some big secret about controlling people's minds. He became very ill because of it, I think he even started believing himself towards the end. Perhaps I shouldn't hate him, perhaps I should pity him.'

I suddenly pitied her, picturing her husband in my mind. She was fairly older than me, but I would have happily taken her away from him. A bit of a belly stretched her purple jumper, but her legs were nice and slim. I thought about what peculiarities may be lurking under her clothing. Things can grow where there was nothing before as you get older.

'Mrs Edwards, is there anyone close to your brother who could have done this, perhaps he'd planned it with them?'

'Well, I had been told by the hospital staff that he'd been getting visits from someone other than me. I asked who, but they wouldn't tell me.'

'A man or a woman?' I asked in haste, believing the identity of the culprit to be in my sights.

'A woman, apparently. Who she is I don't know.'

'I do,' I declared bluntly, rising to my feet.

I knocked at the door pleasantly enough. Barbara Davies answered it.

'Oh, it's you with the push bike!' she said knowingly.

'Yes, it's me. Can I come in?'

'Why, what do you want?' She looked down at me with suspicion. Her eyes felt like pulsars, permeating right through my person.

'I bring good news Miss Davies, very good news indeed,' I fobbed at her.

'Then, you'd better come in,' she said slowly, trying to read my facial expressions. Luckily I was good at appearing bland and expressionless. The door was closed behind me as I passed Barbara in the hallway. I stepped into the living room, but did not sit down this time.

'Inspector Hastings has arrested the murderer,' I told her, looking into her eyes. She did not twitch one bit. She was fixed, solid as a freshly baked conker plastered with vinegar. I was about to drill a hole in her... metaphorically speaking.

'Has he?' she said with a hint of surprise.

'Yes, a Mrs Jane Edwards - sister to the deceased Jason Watkins.'

She looked towards my feet for a second, before once again fixing her piercing stare on my face. My smooth, unhindered face. It had yet to tighten or crease under the ravages of time. 'Really? She lives across the road from the museum, doesn't she?'

'Yes, she does. Apparently she killed Louis Sellers in revenge for putting her brother in prison to die. He died in prison, you know!'

'Really? I didn't know that,' Barbara replied innocently.

'You didn't? Have you ever been to prison, Miss Davies?'

'Of course not,' she replied, surprised by the question.

'That's funny, only you told us yesterday that you'd seen the inside of a prison. Now, who could you have possibly been visiting I wonder?'

Barbara suddenly launched herself at me, taking a firm grip of my neck. We struggled around the room, the attacker becoming ever surer of her actions as she went on at my thin frame. She, her humongous mammary glands rushing around my face as I begged my lungs to draw in air, panted in pleasure. Her nipples, dancing erect together like a ballerina competing with the boogie-woogie, momentarily had me in their hypnotic entrance.

'You'll never get away with it,' I gasped through my closing airway, stamping on her foot and breaking free of her grip. 'Help!' I yelled futilely. Stumbling around a chair, I threw it at her. She knocked it clean out of her way in her quest to silence me. 'They know I'm here, they're on their way.'

'I doubt that, your sort always like to do it themselves. Be the big man. Your mother has told me all about you. Waste of space.'

'Waste of space? I shall have to have a word with her about that!'

'Sad little loner Peter Smith. Hated at school. Never had a girlfriend.'

'Now steady on. Plenty of time for all that yet.'

'Time for you to die.'

Suddenly a knock came at the door.

'Break it down,' I yelled.

'Yeah, he's in there,' Noose called out as he forced the door open. Several officers charged in and took a firm grip of Barbara before she could surprise them. I gave out a huge sigh of relief as they tackled her to the floor.

'Noose, am I glad to see you,' I wheezed, clutching my neck in agony. 'How did you know I was here?'

'Do you think I am so stupid that I don't know what's going on in my own station? You're not so clever you know, the officer who let you in to see Jane Edwards overheard everything and decided he had to report it back to Hastings and me. I presumed you'd once again suspect Barbara Davies. I was prepared for the worst! Thought I'd have to drag you off her, not the other way about.'

'Dear me, it's been a packed morning hasn't it?! Time for some lunch wouldn't you say?' I yawned, flopping down on the sofa, which luckily enough had not been upturned in the struggle. Barbara Davies was lifted to her feet.

'Hey, hey, wait a minute, I want to know what *YOU* know and we don't,' Noose demanded of me.

'I think *SHE* can fill you in now, Inspector. No more games, hey!'

'Alright, alright,' she relented, realising the game was up. 'You know, to sit there and watch an innocent man die, it was terrible. We planned it, you see. I couldn't help it, I fell in love with him. We were going to get married once we'd freed him. If we could have proven his innocence before he died, we'd be together now. But no - you, the police, forced him to die in prison, tortured by a wasted life.'

'He would still have died from the tumour, even if he'd never have gone to prison in the first place!' Noose exclaimed. 'That was in his genetic makeup.'

'He could have lived, damn you.'

'Wait a second, none of this adds up. I mean, why take revenge on the two who had testified against him, surely we would find out in the end?' Noose pondered.

'Being an innocent man in prison makes you do funny things,' Barbara replied.

'Like plotting to get revenge by killing two men? Doesn't sound like an innocent man to me,' I added.

'So you've found Harrington then?'

'Yes, we have,' Noose confirmed, the memory of the horror that met his eyes still fresh in his mind.

'I know what I've done is wrong, but what they did to Jason is wrong. I'm prepared to face my punishment.'

'The irony of all this is, is that Watkins is as guilty as sin itself. You were taken in by a fraudster, a thief and a murderer,' I told her in disgust.

'You're a liar, he was innocent,' Barbara continued to claim.

'If you still believe that, then love is even blinder than I ever imagined.' I stood up and shuffled past the handcuffed Barbara Davies. 'Just one more thing,' I continued, turning to face

Barbara once again, 'who's was the other car you used to go to the museum to kill Sellers? Was it Harrington's?'

'Yes. I walked to Harrington's flat and killed him first. I took his car and headed for the museum. Sellers used to give him a lift to the meetings, so that's why that nosy bitch Jane Edwards didn't recognise it.'

'Must have been a busy night you had,' I replied, tongue firmly in cheek. 'I hope you enjoyed yourself.'

'Not really. It was like sucking on a eunuch's scrotum.'

'I see,' I replied, not knowing for sure at that time what a eunuch actually was... or a scrotum, for that matter. 'Another thing,' I kept on, 'why was Louis Sellers at the museum at such a time of night?'

'Have you ever met his wife? She is intolerable, he slept at the museum most nights after working late. Seems they were a perfect match in my books.' Barbara turned away from me and took one last look around her living room.

'One more thing,' I called to her, mildly curious, 'why mutilate their penises?'

'Why not?'

'It appears that Barbara Davies only started going to see Watkins in the last year. She had found out about the murder that occurred before she joined, and wanted to write a book about it! She went to meet Watkins in prison, and the rest, as they say, is history!' Noose sighed. 'She also rang her house with Louis Sellers' mobile phone after she murdered him, to make it look authentic.'

'Fascinating,' I replied, focusing my attentions on Hastings and his fish. 'You know, Inspector, you really have some nice fish in this tank,' I complimented him, following the fish as they swam around the tank. Suddenly, the office door swung open. In stepped the superintendent.

'Ah, Super... Superintendent!' Hastings stuttered, surprised to see his superior back already. 'You're back early, it's only half four.' He checked his watch nervously, tapping at its face.

'Yes Hastings, I couldn't resist it when I heard about the horrific murders being committed here. I decided I must come and help, only I come back to find everything wrapped up.' She smiled, predicting Hastings' response.

'Everything wrapped up? Well of course!' he replied, wary of his superior's tricks.

'Everything? Not quite everything though, Hastings, you little worm. What is this I hear about a missing murder weapon?'

'A missing murder weapon? I don't know what you mean, Superintendent,' he whimpered innocently, slouching.

'Oh, and this official complaint made against you! Come now, tell all.'

'I think this is my cue to leave,' I chuckled under my breath, quietly slipping past Noose.

'I can explain everything, Superintendent,' Hastings went on, 'you must ask Henry, he knows...'

I walked into the living room and sat down on the sofa across from Mother in her armchair.

'Aunt Sally didn't know Barbara Davies that well, did she?' I announced over the sound of the TV. 'Anything good on?' I asked.

'A murder mystery,' Mother replied, her eyes fixed on the screen.

'Really? I like a mystery.' Silence. 'Barbara Davies did it after all,' I reported.

'Does that mean I'll get my Sheffield steel spoons back?'

The next day I felt compelled to go to the museum. I don't know why, as I always try not to get myself involved in things. But, on this occasion I walked straight in and discovered a meeting of the Museum Club was in progress. I could hear the voices pulsating from the room, though not exactly what they were saying. As I tried the door, I discovered it was locked. Quickly I turned and walked away, only to hear the sound of the door unlocking. I stopped and turned to see a man's face poking out. 'Peter Smith,' he spoke gently.

'Yes. How do you know who I am?'

'We've been expecting you.'

'Who has?'

'The Museum Club.'

'Oh. And who are you?'

'You will never know my name, nor the names of the other members.'

'That puts me at a disadvantage.'

'On the contrary.'

'I know the names of two members already... past members - Louis Sellers and James Harrington.'

He laughed. 'They were not members of *OUR* Museum Club. Come, join us. We have much to discuss.'

I went inside.

11PM NEWS: TONIGHT

'Neville Jeffries, who appeared on this very sofa earlier this evening, committed suicide live on television an hour ago. Claiming to be the author of the now controversial book *I AM DEAD*, credited to Peter Smith, he promised to rise again as a messianic figure who will guide us all to some sort of salvation - salvation that remains unspecified. He has yet to do so, and has largely been vilified online. A storm has arisen, with download sales of his book hitting the one million mark since the broadcast ended. In the book, which I am also currently reading, a policy known as the dignity experiment is passed as law in which elderly people are encouraged to sign up. The law takes care of the elderly when they reach a certain age, allowing the government to cut the cost of healthcare and paying pensions. The Prime Minister, who initially refused to get involved in the live suicide, has since been discussing the dignity experiment:'

PM'S OPINION:

'Let us not judge a book by its cover, so to speak. Let us not judge at all. Ours is not the place to judge. Ours is the place to understand the wishes of the individual. Yes, a nation just took part in one man's suicide. And yet, that is wholly within the law - the law that you all took part in deciding with the recent referendum on assisted dying. We, as a nation, have united over this matter - a matter of coming together, joining hands and making our minds up. Where Peter Smith, the author of this book,' The PM holds up a copy of *I AM DEAD*, 'is right now remains a mystery to the authorities - but his message is ever present. His message, delivered by Neville, discusses a vast swathe of things. One thing, of course, is dignity. We, the government, want dignity for all. More specifically, we want dignity for the vulnerable members of society - the elderly, the disabled - will all receive *DIGNITY* from us. You can trust us to do the right thing on your behalf.'

BACK IN THE STUDIO:

'The Prime Minister there, of course, admitting that the whereabouts of the actual Peter Smith remain a mystery. Now, one woman, who is calling herself the first Elder Icon, says she is dedicated to spreading the word of Peter Smith and building his following in the wake of Neville's death. She joins us now, live from Harnlan.' Richard turns to face the screen, which is filled with the image of a rather pale and gaunt Sharon. She stares into the camera, her withdrawn eyes drooping down towards her withered, sunken cheeks.

'Everything is nothing,' she starts.

'Turn that TV off, Mr Monkey,' Gerty demanded of her fleecy companion in the camper. 'I shan't tell you again.'

'But, Mrs Hinklebottom, it's all about that Neville who used to travel with us all those years ago,' the puppet protested. 'He's just done himself in on the telly!'

'What an attention-seeking cretin! Never liked him. Now,' she continued, 'to bed. We have a busy day of crime-fighting ahead of us come morn.'

The PM walked into his bedroom, where his wife was busy putting on a shiny black twelve inch strap-on. He slipped his dressing gown off, hanging it on a little hook on the back of the door, and dropped his underpants down to the floor. Manoeuvring his legs out of them, he kicked them to one side and made for the bed, pulling the duvet cover back. 'Good idea, this dignity thing. It's going to solve a lot of debt problems. We'll work out some spin on it in the morning, get the peasants onboard.'

His wife, the massive dildo now protruding from her as her exposed breasts lopped lazily either side of it, picked up a tube of lube off the dressing table.

'No,' instructed the PM, 'don't lube up tonight. I want this to sting,' he sighed as he wrapped a belt around his neck and pulled tight on it, getting down on all fours on the bed and pulling his bum cheeks apart. 'Safe word... Eurozone.'

She came down on him like a tonne of bricks, slamming his head down onto the mattress and forcing the dry, rigid dildo deep into his blistered anus as she pulled hard on the end of the belt. Blood and poo gushed forth as he moaned and groaned, digging his blazing white teeth into the pillow and not quite knowing whether he was in searing agony or sheer joy.

MRS HINKLEBOTTOM AND MR MONKEY IN: THE COPYCAT CLOWN

The primary school car park was empty, quiet and serene. All the kids were busy inside the quaint stone building, the gentle singing of morning hymns emanating from within. Hopscotch brightened up the tarmac yard, a wooden board with a mother and child painted on it standing at the end of three disabled parking spaces. Suddenly Gerty's campervan slammed into the board, stopping over all three spaces. The driver's door swung open and a cigarette stub with lipstick on the end dropped to the ground. A slippered foot slipped out and stamped on it, before being joined by a second foot. Next, an umbrella walking stick joined them as the passenger door opened. Two orange furry paws dropped out that side, dangling from thin cloth legs.

'We have him cornered this time,' Gerty purred, raising a finger into the air as the pair trundled towards the school.

A villainous fiend, known only as The Clown - owing to his drab costume and sometime profession as a children's entertainer - was busy blowing a party whistle and folding balloons in front of a class of eight year old children. Some seemed to be enjoying it, others yawned - yet more were rather fearful. After all, this *WAS* a clown. The door swung open and Gerty stepped in.

'Your time's up, Clown.'

The Clown turned to meet his arch nemesis, his party whistle drooping in his mouth. Mr Monkey appeared from behind the doorframe and chuckled.

'You're doomed! DOOMED!' laughed the puppet.

'I don't think so,' The Clown replied in haste, 'for I have outwitted you this time!'

He clicked his fingers and the children all got to their feet, arms outstretched towards the crime-fighting duo as they chanted: 'Kill, kill, kill!'

'Oh no!' Mr Monkey gulped.

'It appears The Clown has harnessed mind control and turned these children into OAP-consuming zombies,' Gerty cried in horror.

'*WE'RE* doomed! DOOMED!' Mr Monkey yelled... 'DOOMED!!!'

'Hmm,' Gerty thought, 'not if I know balloon-folding.' She grabbed the longest balloon she could find and charged at The Clown, wrapping it around his neck and twisting it tightly. The pair grappled, but the paler of the two managed to pick a hair pin from the elder's bouffant and popped the balloon around his neck. He squirted water at her from the flower on his lapel before making for the window.

'You will never foil my clown-related antics, old hag!' he cackled, before leaping at the closed window. It shattered as his girth pounded through.

'After him, Mrs Hinklebottom!' Mr Monkey called out.

A child grabbed hold of her leg and she looked down at him in disappointment. 'In my day we got a smack.' She looked back at the smashed window, tutting. 'You just applied your last layer of makeup, Clown.'

'Ooo, I like that one,' Mr Monkey howled with laughter. 'Yes, that's a good one.'

Shaking the naughty boy off, Gerty marched up to the window and climbed through onto the school yard as a multicoloured reliant robin spun past, driving off into the distance with its comical horn blaring a cacophony of obscenely high-pitched circus tunes whilst party poppers exploded all around.

The old woman and her puppet pal were in hot pursuit in their camper. The Clown was eager to make a menace of himself, winding in and out of traffic on the busy road.

'You take the wheel,' Gerty told Mr Monkey as a thought crossed her mind.

'But what about my driving ban?'

She slid the sunroof open and stepped onto her seat as he grabbed hold of the wheel with his mouth. 'Now's not the time to worry about breaking the law,' she responded, her head poking out of the sunroof. Mr Monkey breathed a sigh of relief. 'I'll simply have you charged later.' Mr Monkey groaned. She hauled herself up onto the roof of the speeding vehicle as it neared The Clown's three-wheeler, clutching ever tighter onto her handbag. The Clown looked out of his rear view mirror and spotted the persistent pensioner waving her fist at him.

The two vehicles touched and Gerty seized her chance, leaping off her roof and onto The Clown's. She shimmied forward and poked her face down to look at him through the windscreen. He swung about, turning his window wipers on, trying everything his imagination could muster in order to get her off. However, she brandished a hammer and smashed the glass.

'Die you old bitch, DIE!' he spat, trying to punch her. She opened her handbag, throwing out a brush and a bag of humbugs before finding a can of mace.

'As my husband could well attest,' she announced, 'if you interfere with me, you'll get a face full of mace.' She sprayed his eyes and he squealed in agony as the vehicle spun out of control and careered off the road.

Inspector Kennedy strode up to the police station reception desk and smiled at the young receptionist. She appeared somewhat flustered, trying to straighten her ruffled brown hair as Kennedy said: 'Good morning! Lovely day!' She nodded as mumblings came from beneath her. Gerty appeared behind the inspector, miraculously unscathed by the happenings a day prior. She gave out a little lady's cough. Kennedy's face soured and his head dropped. 'Hinklebottom,' he moaned.

'*MRS* Hinklebottom to you, Inspector Kennedy. My marital status shall not be ignored.' She lifted her leg onto the skirting of the reception desk, revealing her suspenders. 'I shan't have some randy copper sniffing around my turf.' Kennedy heaved, trying with all his might to swallow the bit of sick now in his mouth. 'Anyway, we caught The Clown.'

'You what?' he fired back, incensed.

'That's right,' she answered, grinning, 'Mr Monkey and I.' The puppet appeared from underneath the reception desk as the receptionist blushed. 'No thanks to you, Inspector! Anyway, chop chop, Mr Monkey, we have a jigsaw to complete.'

Mr Monkey made his way to his boss, who was now waiting for him in the doorway. The receptionist looked longingly after him. He paused in the door, turning briefly to face her. 'I'll email,' he told her, sniggering a bit. 'Sometime.'

She flopped back in her seat, overcome.

It was now evening and the camper was parked up in a lay-by, a light on in the back. Inside, Gerty and Mr Monkey had made things very homely. She was preparing for bed, the sofa at the back all pulled out and covered with a nice flowery duvet. She pulled it back and moved her hot water bottle from the top to the bottom, before sitting on the edge and putting some bed socks on.

'Wonderful day in work today, Raymond... Yes, we caught The Clown.' She turned to look at the other side of the bed, where her husband's urn was tucked safely in. 'I know, I know... I'm getting older now and I realise that. But, with the police being so cack-handed and arse-about-face, this world needs me.' She picked up a glass of water off the windowsill and took a sip from it. 'Without me, children's entertainers would be running amok in our primary schools. Ah well, time for bed I suppose.' She got into bed and tucked herself in, leaning over and giving the urn a kiss. 'Goodnight, Raymond. Sweet dreams.' She leant over to the side of the bed and looked down. There lay Mr Monkey, his head poking out of a shoebox under the bed. 'Goodnight, Mr Monkey.'

'Night, night, Mrs Hinklebottom,' he yawned back.

'But no sweet dreams for you, because you are a puppet and have no soul,' she told him as she fixed the lid on the shoebox. He sighed from within his sealed container. She lay back and rested her head on the pillow. 'Oh yes, and I nearly forgot about you driving while disqualified. Must sort that out in the morning!' There came more sighing from poor Mr Monkey as she turned the bedside lamp off.

The next morning Gerty and Mr Monkey made their way down the street on their way to the shops.

'Another glorious day!' Mr Monkey declared. 'Not a cloud in the sky, nor a vagabond or ruffian in sight.'

'A quick trip to the shop and back in time for a slice of Swiss roll. If only every day could be this perfect!' Gerty concurred.

'And maybe I'll catch up with that receptionist a bit later,' Mr Monkey thought aloud. He would have scratched his chin, if he had a chin, or hands for that matter. He had paws, yes, and these currently hung by his sides, swinging lifelessly as he bobbed along.

Gerty spotted something in the distance.

'Over there, look! What's all that hubbub outside the newsagents?'

'Well bugger me!' was Mr Monkey's reply as he spotted the place covered in police tape.

'Language! Buggery is no joke, Mr Monkey. It is a heinous crime... Anyway, come on!' An old man rode past on a mobility scooter. Gerty stepped in his way. 'Halt! I am reprimanding this vehicle.' She pushed him off and jumped on, Mr Monkey jumping behind and holding on as though he was on a motorbike. They rode off, slowly, towards the newsagents.

'Reprimanding?' Mr Monkey questioned.

Inside the shop, Kennedy examined the corpse of the middle-aged male shopkeeper, lying strewn behind the counter. The victim, a chalk mark drawn around him, had balloon animal parts protruding from his eyes, nose, mouth, ears and groin. Gerty and Mr Monkey drove through the police tape and approached the scene as Kennedy addressed an officer: 'Hmm. Balloon animal asphyxiation. Worst case I've ever seen.' He caught sight of the crime-fighting duo ahead and pointed angrily at them. 'YOU! You said you'd brought in The Clown! If he's in custody, then who's done this?'

'Oh my,' Gerty puzzled, upset. 'I don't understand.'

'Is this a joke to you, Hinklebottom?' Kennedy raged. 'Every orifice in this man's body has been penetrated by balloon animals! You think that's funny?!'

Mr Monkey chuckled.

'Now steady on! I'm sure there's a rational explanation.' Her eyes darted about the shop as she tapped her chin. 'Have you checked the vicinity for zombie children?' Kennedy scowled at her. 'The man you have in custody IS The Clown. I'd stake my reputation on it. Both myself and my puppet sidekick have seen his crimes with our own eyes.'

'Mine are buttons,' Mr Monkey chirped.

'Get out of here, Hinklebottom! This is a serious case, and we don't need your shenanigans interfering with proper police work.' He gestured towards an officer, beckoning him over.

'Sullivan, get over here and help me extract the giraffe from this man's rectum.'

Gerty and Mr Monkey, deflated, left.

'I just don't understand it,' she lamented.

'What, decimalisation?' Mr Monkey asked glibly.

'No, no, this murder - it has all the calling cards of The Clown, but he's behind bars. There's only one possibility.' Her eyes widened as she grimaced. 'We have a copycat - a copycat clown!'

'Well bugger me!'

Gerty gave the poor puppet a whack across the back of the head.

The newspaper headlines were typically playful, the best being "Clown in Custardy". The random murders continued, Gerty and Mr Monkey looking on in horror as more victims were killed in clownish ways - one was discovered lying flat on his stomach, his face submerged in a cream pie, and another was hanging from a load of colourful balloons.

The duo stormed into the police station. The receptionist blushed and twiddled her hair. 'I haven't received your email yet, Mr Monkey,' she said.

'Haven't you?' responded the cloth primate sheepishly.

'Where's The Clown?' Gerty demanded, banging her fist on the desk. Kennedy appeared.

'My, er...' Mr Monkey stuttered as the young woman fluttered her eyelashes at him. 'My internet is down.'

'Is it? It was working alright this morning when I had my pre-breakfast gambling session,' Gerty pointed out to the puppet.

'Oh, er...'

'I thought I told you to stay away,' Kennedy roared at them.

Gerty, ignoring his indignation, pushed him aside and marched through the double doors leading to the cells.

Handcuffed, The Clown was thrown down onto the hard plastic chair where an intense light was shone in his eyes. He struggled to turn away from it, but Gerty stepped up close behind him and slammed his face onto the table. His big red clown nose honked.

'Owwww! Look what you did! Now my nose is all red!' he chuckled at his interrogator.

She pulled a chair out, turning it around and sitting on it so that the back was facing the front. Lighting a cigarette in a holder, she rested her arms on the top of the chair.

Meanwhile, Kennedy and Mr Monkey watched through the one-way mirror.

'Oh dear, oh dear!' Mr Monkey whispered. 'She's done the chair thing. He's in for it now.'

The Clown looked pretty smug, even spitting on the floor as Gerty blew smoke in his face.

'Who's the Copycat Clown?' she demanded of this misfit.

'Want to sniff my flower?' he joked, twitching his own nose towards the plastic flower on his lapel.

'There's somebody copying your crimes.'

'It's a really nice flower. Go on, sniff it.'

Gerty leant forward, grabbing hold of and twisting The Clown's big curly red hair, causing him considerable pain. 'Don't be facetious!' she demanded. 'Who is it?'

'How should I know?'

'Tell me!' she yelled, grabbing hold of his big red nose and twisting it. He cried out in more pain as it honked again.

'Honestly, I don't know,' he cried. Gerty glared at him. 'It could be the guy who runs my fan club, though.'

'You have a fan club?'

'Of course. The Clown's Club. 26 members - active members,' The Clown gloated proudly.

'And where can I find this fiendish clown fetishist?'

Meanwhile, the other side of the one-way mirror, Mr Monkey laughed. 'She's damn good, ain't she?'

Kennedy rolled his eyes.

'And if I ask you something again, you tell me right away. Got it?' Gerty carried on at the powdered villain.

'Why, what are you gonna do if I don't - put me in one of your marmalades?'

There was a loud bang as blood splattered on the mirror. A horn sounded as a penny whistle played. The Clown groaned.

'How on earth can you live with this woman?' Kennedy asked the furry puppet in fury.

Mr Monkey turned aside, looking down contemplatively. 'It's a long story, Inspector. A very long one.'

'Oh?'

'Yup,' Mr Monkey replied, turning back and moving right up to Kennedy's face.

'Keep up, Mr Monkey!' Gerty called back as she stormed out of the station. He, meanwhile, bumped into the receptionist.

'Oh, Mr Monkey! You've been ignoring me since last we embraced,' she gushed at him. He looked blankly back at her. 'Please, just give it to me straight - I need to know how you feel about me.'

'Okay, er, receptionist lady - if that IS your real name - It's all just a rich tapestry of sizzling emotions and stuff, isn't it. It's, it's...'

She took hold of his floppy paw. 'I have such strong feelings for you. And yet... and yet I feel I don't even know you. You're a mystery to me - a mystery wrapped in an enigma, wrapped in a 60% polyester, 40% cotton orange sleeve.'

'There really isn't that much to know... really.'

She yanked him closer. 'Let me inside you. Let me know who you really are.'

He gulped. 'Well, okay. I suppose I could tell you my life story in song form.' He cleared his throat. 'My name is Mr Monkey,' he sang in an angelic alto, 'I live in a camper, with an O-A-P...' Images of his past flashed in his memory as he continued: 'Once I was married to an ex-porn star... Married for seven whole years!' Visions of Jane Jenkins, a clearly middle-aged woman with bleach-blonde hair and an ample bosom and wearing a revealing black PVC catsuit, quickly stepped out of a limousine and posed for the paparazzi as Mr Monkey popped his head out of the window, ignored. 'Now all day I just sit on my rear end... Standing up to scratch it infrequently.' A beer can in his paw, he sat slumped in the camper watching kids TV. Next to him was Gerty, fast asleep, her mouth wide open and her top false teeth fallen down. 'My trivial life was once great... Starring in a string of hit movies.' Now Mr Monkey envisioned his time on movie sets in the dim and distant past, even accepting awards at ceremonies and having his photo taken with other A-listers. 'Then one day I happened to go ape-shit... Unfairly arrested, I fell from grace.' He attacked the cameraman on the film set, banging his own head against the wall, and assaulted his celebrity friends. Such cruel, cruel memories. 'What is a monkey to do?' he continued singing, turning back to face the receptionist as his memories faded once more. 'Only a puppet... And orange too!' He put his paw on her shoulder. 'So there you go,' he now spoke, 'a little snippet into my background. A little taster, if you wish.'

However, the receptionist stepped back. 'A porn star?'

'*EX*-porn star... Didn't I do well!' he sniggered. She slapped him across the face.

'Oh God, oh God. I'll have to go and have myself checked out. I feel... I feel so dirty,' she sobbed, running off. Mr Monkey, now alone, looked awkwardly around the room.

'Yup, the ladies certainly do love a puppet monkey such as myself.'

Gerty spotted the semi-detached house up ahead and smashed through the fence, slamming the breaks on the camper right on top of the garden. Plants were crushed, gnomes were decapitated. She stepped out, crushing a gnome's head under her slipper. She stormed at the door, kicking it and grabbing at the handle until it flew open. A middle-aged couple were sitting just inside, eating TV dinners on the sofa, and fearfully looked up at the angry octogenarian.

'Where is he?' she yelled.

The man, eyes on Gerty the whole time, sliced into a sausage and, placing it in his mouth, proceeded to chew it very slowly.

Upstairs was Justin, the target of Gerty's rage. An obese chap in his late 20s, he was busy sitting at his desk in his bedroom with his penis in his hand. He wanked and yawned, a resigned look on his face as he stared at an unfolding music video on his laptop screen. Suddenly Gerty stormed in, demanding: 'Are you Justin Bates?'

A little flustered, he ejaculated and quickly shut the lid of his laptop.

'No. I am Justin Bates BSc.,' he responded.

'I don't care what degree you have,' she shouted, clacking him across the back of the head. 'Put your dick away, you dirty little boy.'

'I got a 2:1.'

'Do you run The Clown's fan club?' Gerty pushed, twisting his ear.

'Yes, yes,' he squirmed. She released his ear. 'I started, as a social experiment, an internet fan club for The Clown.'

'Whatever for?'

'I reasoned that the only people who'd join would be psychopaths. Thus, I could pinpoint potential future, or present, psychopaths.'

Gerty slapped a pair of handcuffs on him. 'You're nicked.'

'Mind if I wash my hands?'

Justin was suspended by his wrists from a chain hooked to the ceiling of the camper. The curtains were drawn, and Gerty paced around the tubby drooper with a knuckle duster as blood trickled from his nose and his black eyes stung.

'Please, I know nothing,' he tried to tell her. She was having none of it.

'I shan't ask again.' She adjusted the knuckle duster, ready to do more damage.

'Look, I told you... it's just a social experiment. I'm trying to solve crimes. I'm just like you.'

Gerty stopped dead, horrified at the mere suggestion they were the same. She stepped slowly up to him and grabbed hold of his cheeks, leaning in until their faces were almost touching.

'Just like me? Just like *ME*? How *DARE* you.'

Justin found himself overwhelmed by her breath, trying desperately to get away. 'Maybe I was a little hasty,' he gasped. 'I'm not a lover of fish, for example.'

She let him go, stepping back once more. He gasped for fresh air, coughing up a little bit of sick. Gerty shook her head in disappointment. Suddenly Mr Monkey appeared over Justin's shoulder. 'Come now, Mrs Hinklebottom! Can't you see the boy is confused and upset?' the puppet laughed.

She spun back around and leant right into Justin's face once more, breathing down his mouth. He gasped for air, his nostrils dilating and blood vessels exploding in his eyes as he struggled for clean air.

'All I can see is a copycat clown,' she grunted, turning away in disgust. Justin breathed out, turning to Mr Monkey.

'God sake, can't you smell it?' he asked the puppet.

'No. I don't have a real nose,' he replied. 'It's just a piece of cotton.'

'Wait, did you say copycat clown?' Justin asked, turning to Gerty.

'Yes. Somebody is copying The Clown's gruesome methods of murder.' She leant in yet again. 'You!'

'No, not me. But... but I might just know who!'

Gerty, one hand on the steering wheel and the other clutching a fish sandwich, swerved the camper in and out of traffic as Justin sat next to her, bound in reams and reams of cheap yellow sticky tape. Mr Monkey was poking his head through the curtain behind the pair.

'Yes, he joined the club about a week or so ago - said he wanted to copy everything The Clown did,' Justin explained. Gerty took her eyes off the road and leant towards the lad, waving the half-eaten butty in his face.

'Want a bite?' she asked the quivering wreck. The camper swerved into oncoming traffic as she took one last bite before putting the remains in the glove box - alongside half-eaten biscuits, a mouldy banana and a grenade. A car blared its horn, ending up in the ditch as the camper carried on ploughing forward.

'Ah, here we are,' Justin called out, spotting the house up ahead. 'This is where I tracked him down to.' Gerty slammed the breaks on and Justin lunged forward, banging his head on the windscreen.

'You had better be right, Justin... or else...'

There was a prolonged pause as she stared at him.

'Or else what?' he finally relented. Gerty turned to Mr Monkey, before looking back at Justin.

'Or else, the next sandwich I eat won't have fish on it...'

'Thank God for that,' Justin sighed in relief.

'It will have *YOU* on it,' she threatened, pressing a finger into his stomach. Justin looked confused as Gerty stepped out of the camper and approached the house. He turned to the puppet.

'Say, Mr Monkey, you couldn't just loosen this tape a bit could you? I don't see why I have to be bound like this.'

'Wait a minute! If I do, are you going to try and escape?'

'Of course not!'

'Well that's alright then.' He pulled at the tape with his mouth.

Gerty slowly opened the door and gingerly stepped inside the creepy old house.

'Door ajar upon arrival,' she spoke into a handheld voice recorder. 'Seemingly deserted.'

'Hello!' Mr Monkey shouted out, appearing from behind Gerty. 'Anyone in?' Gerty grabbed hold of his mouth to shut him up.

The hallway was dark and misty. Mr Monkey moved into the living room as Gerty started walking slowly up the stairs. She opened her handbag, taking out a small folded umbrella, extending and holding it out as a makeshift weapon.

Meanwhile, Mr Monkey looked around the living room, a plethora of clown-related items filling it. Suddenly Gerty screamed from upstairs.

A shady figure rushed past in the hallway and out through the front door as Mr Monkey darted to Gerty's aid. She, lying on the floor upstairs, gave out a little cough.

'Oh no! Are you okay, Mrs Hinklebottom?!'

'Somebody caught me off-guard.' She coughed again. A hoarse kind of cough. 'Knocked me for six. Go after them, Mr Monkey.'

'They'll have gone by now. I'm more concerned about you! Have you broken a hip or anything?'

Gerty whacked him with her bag, knocking him against a door, which swung open. She turned to look into the room, aghast with horror at what lay inside. Opening her handbag, and rooting around in it, she brought out a photograph. She held it up, looking into the room.

'That's our supposed copycat clown.'

'Dear lord. Is it?' Mr Monkey responded, turning to have a look at the mess.

'Yes,' Gerty replied, 'I can just about make out his outlandishly small hat under all that silly string.'

'Ooo, look!' Mr Monkey exclaimed, pointing up at the wall. Somebody had written "NO MORE CLOWNING AROUND, HINKLEBOTTOM" in blood on it.

'How *DARE* they not pre-fix a Mrs to that! Anyone would think I wasn't legally entitled to half of Raymond's private pension!'

'I thought you pretended he was still alive in order to claim it all,' Mr Monkey suggested as Gerty hastily struggled to her feet.

'Now is *NOT* the time for tittle-tattle, Monkey.'

'Er, excuse me... *MR* Monkey!'

Gerty limped down the stairs. 'So, the man Justin thought was our man isn't our man.'

'He's no longer a man at all if my button eyes didn't just deceive me,' Mr Monkey giggled, musing over the image of the man's mutilated body.

Gerty, now at the bottom, shouted up at her assistant: 'Stop ruminating, and get down these stairs at once!'

'He's not our man, Justin,' Gerty extrapolated as she and Mr Monkey got back into the camper.

'He's nobody's man now,' Mr Monkey laughed. 'It's all just a bit of goo now.'

'Justin, I am speaking to you!' Gerty seethed, turning to see that he had gone. 'Well bugger me!'

'Er, yes. Quite right,' Mr Monkey stuttered.

'But how on earth did he get free? I bound him myself.'

'Beats me,' Mr Monkey replied, turning away and whistling.

'Justin *MUST* be our killer. No doubt he quickly broke free somehow, got in the house whilst you weren't looking, knocked me out, did the murder to silence the man who isn't our man, then made a break for it.' She looked down, disappointed in herself. 'Oh, Mr Monkey, this is all very upsetting.' She removed a hanky from up her cardigan sleeve and blew her nose.

'I know, I know. I'm very upset at all these innocent people being murdered in cold blood too,' Mr Monkey lamented.

'No, it's not that - it's so upsetting that I let the murderer escape. I trusted what he told me. I have failed.'

Mr Monkey put his paw on her shoulder. 'Oh, come now Mrs Hinklebottom, don't beat yourself up about it... Though yes, it is clearly your fault and I did not in any way loosen Justin's binds which aided in his escape.'

'Oh well,' Gerty sniffled, 'time to go and face the music, I suppose. Inspector Kennedy is really going to enjoy this.'

The receptionist looked disparagingly across at Mr Monkey as he followed Gerty towards the double doors. They were headed for Kennedy's office, and nothing was going to stop them.

'Inspector, I need a word,' Gerty shouted out as she banged on his door in the corridor. There was no reply. She banged again, followed by more screeching, as Mr Monkey peeped through the keyhole. Suddenly the door opened. 'Ah, Inspector.'

'Save it, you interfering old bat. I've heard it all before,' he grunted back.

'No. I, I just came to...' she looked down, withdrawn. 'I came to apologise.'

'You what?' Kennedy spat, his jaw dropping.

'Yes. I'm sorry Inspector, I allowed the Copycat Clown to escape.' A tear rolled down her cheek.

'I see,' Kennedy replied gleefully.

'Please, don't beg me to stay on as your assistant. It's better I went. I've slipped up this time, allowing a serial killer to run free. Next time I may slip up much worse.'

'Yes, you might slip on a banana skin and break your hip,' Mr Monkey pointed out.

'Well, what can I say?' Kennedy responded, a huge smile on his face. 'I accept your apology, and resignation from bugging me - forthwith.'

'Thank you, Inspector.' She turned to leave. 'Thank you for your understanding at this time. I know we haven't always seen eye to eye, especially since you're a foot taller than I, but I'd like to think we became friends as well as colleagues.'

'Yes,' Kennedy chuckled, rubbing his hands together. Gerty walked away, followed by her faithful puppet pal. Suddenly, however, she stopped and turned back.

'Oh, Inspector, I couldn't just ask one last favour could I - seeing as I am going, never ever to return?'

'I suppose,' he sighed. 'What is it?'

'I couldn't see The Clown one last time, could I? I just want to look him in the eye one last time, for old time's sake. Would you mind ever so much?'

'Very well.'

The Clown was lying on the bed in the station cell, reading a copy of CRIME AND PUNISHMENT. He gave out a little yawn, turning the page as Gerty entered. Without looking up, he sniffed the air and greeted her with: 'Gertrude Hinklebottom, how good of you to come.'

'This is just a social call, Clown. I'm off the case. Off any case for good, now. Retiring.' She gave out a little cough. Perhaps forced at first, it turned into something quite tricky to shake off as she had a prolonged coughing fit.

'Really? I am sorry to hear that. Better get that cough sorted out too.' He sat up. 'You made a formidable foe. But, everything must come to an end... in the end.'

'Yes, you're right,' she replied through the coughing. Turning to leave, she pulled her foot up and found a piece of sticky tape stuck to it. She bent down and picked it off her slipper, examining it - the same sticky tape she'd used to bind Justin. She knew it was, it was the horrible dark yellow tape from a pound shop. All those years of being tight with her money had paid off.

Slowly she turned to The Clown, looking at his hands. There was more tape on one of his cuffs. She pulled it off, gasping: 'You did it! *YOU* are your own copycat! You took Justin from my campervan!' The Clown smiled as the realisation registered on her face and made it look like a desiccated piece of discarded leather. 'But how? You're in here.'

Slow clapping came from behind. She turned to see Kennedy applauding.

'Congratulations, Hinklebottom. You just couldn't leave it alone, could you?'

'*YOU*? You let him out to commit these murders? Oh the horror! Why?'

'Who cares? I suppose it got you to leave. Well, almost.'

'Leaving is something I shall be doing right now,' she proclaimed, trying to step around Kennedy. He burst into laughter.

'I'm afraid I can't let that happen now. You simply know too much,' he told her as he moved in, pushing her into The Clown's grasp, who thrashed her across the head, knocking her unconscious.

The receptionist was trying her utmost best to ignore Mr Monkey, who was trying desperately to get her attention.

'Oh come on, sweet cheeks! Chuckle butty! Remember the good times we shared?' he trilled at her.

Meanwhile, in the background, Kennedy pushed a large laundry basket towards the exit.

Nighttime had, like clockwork, come yet again and Kennedy and The Clown were in their evil secret hideout - Kennedy's cellar. All manner of hideous items hung from the brown, earthy walls: clown wigs, over-sized shoes, even baggy trousers. The Clown was sitting at a pink dressing table reapplying his makeup, the mirror surrounded by a few working lights and some broken bulbs. Behind him, tied to chairs, were Gerty and Justin.

'I've been waiting for this for so long,' Kennedy purred, appearing through the heavy red door. 'Oh the pain and suffering you have caused me.' He slipped his cat mask on and got down on all fours, rolling onto his back and outstretching his legs and arms.

'Aww!' The Clown replied, rushing over and tickling Kennedy's stomach. 'Stretch a big pussy.'

Gerty looked over at Justin, who was absolutely shitting himself in fear. 'We've had it. This is endgame, my boy. Sorry for getting you involved,' she said to him. He screamed out in terror and sorrow.

'Sorry?' Kennedy laughed, getting to his feet and storming over to Gerty. 'Everybody's always sorry, aren't they? Bull fucking shit are they sorry!' he stormed.

'What on earth brought about this alteration in you, Inspector?' Gerty shot back, shaking her head in disappointment.

'This *IS* me,' he proclaimed confidently. 'There's always two sides to the coin. That's just how things are.'

'But,' she kept on, 'surely something turned you into this monster presently before me?'

'Have you never done wicked things, old one?' he asked her. Of course she had. Were they the same?

'Enough!' The Clown interrupted. 'It doesn't matter how or why we all ended up like we are. All that matters is that we're all here now, and I have a wicked and sadistic end for all three of you.'

'Three? But I only count two,' Kennedy responded, turning to face The Clown. He was met with a puff of smoke from a ring on The Clown's finger and collapsed to the floor unconscious.

'Now,' The Clown started, 'let's see. For you, Gertrude, I have a very slow and agonising death planned to reflect the strife you have caused me during my entire reign of criminal activity.' He pressed a button on one of his other rings. A section of the wall behind him turned around, revealing a toilet. There was an awkward, confused silence. Sensing an issue, he eventually turned around to face the toilet.

'Wrong button?' Gerty laughed.

'No!'

'So my death involves a toilet?'

'You will be starved of your daily box of diarrhoea tablets, left down here to fester with only rich cream pies to eat and a toilet that doesn't flush!' he cackled, rubbing his hands together in glee. Gerty just raised an eyebrow in response.

'What about me?' Justin asked, a tremor of fear in his voice.

The Clown burst out into yet more laughter, skipping over to a curtain. 'You, my fat ugly fan, shall become a balloon!' He pulled the curtain open, revealing a makeshift balloon pump attached to a gas canister. On the end of the nozzle was what appeared to be a normal deflated balloon. As The Clown turned the gas on and it inflated the balloon, it became clear this was not normal at all. It was made of human skin, with the face still visible. The eyes, nose and mouth had been sealed shut and the greasy hair moved about only a little bit as the head got bigger and bigger. Suddenly it popped, splattering the dead face skin all over everyone. Justin screamed and screamed, begging to be freed. The Clown just laughed.

'Did anyone order a pizza?' a somewhat muffled Mr Monkey suddenly asked. The gathering turned to the red door, where Mr Monkey had miraculously appeared, holding a pizza box in his mouth.

'Mr Monkey!' Gerty sighed in relief.

'What?' The Clown begged in surprise.

Mr Monkey dropped the pizza box on the floor. 'I said, did anyone order a pizza?' The Clown grabbed hold of a baseball bat and charged at the puppet with it. 'Oh crumbs!' Mr Monkey gasped, leaping out of the way and disappearing behind the balloon pump. The Clown turned and darted at it, where a semi-conscious Kennedy stuck his foot into the air and tripped him up. The Clown fell mouth first onto the pump and Mr Monkey turned it on with his own mouth. The Clown's mouth quickly filled with the gas.

'Oh no! Hoist by my own petard!' he puffed as his entire head quickly inflated, exploding around the room with an almighty "POP".

'Try and fold *THAT* balloon, scumbag,' was Mr Monkey's triumphant response.

'But, Mr Monkey, I still don't understand how you knew where we were,' Gerty again mused, scratching her hairy chin as she and her pal lazed on the deck chairs outside the camper.

'Well, when I saw that you, the Inspector and The Clown were all missing I put two and two together and knew he must have escaped and taken you hostage. I never possibly imagined the Inspector would turn out to be a crook, though!'

'Yes, yes,' Gerty replied, 'but how did you discover our location?'

'I'm getting to that!'

You see, I was still being ignored by that hot receptionist who I was trying to woo back.

'Oh come on,' I said, 'I'm trying my best here. I've even got you a surprise.'

'Oh?' she replied, very pleased indeed.

'Yes, it'll be here any minute now.' And it was, as suddenly a pizza boy walked in, carrying a pizza box. 'Well would you believe it, here we are!' Impeccable timing, don't you think?

'My surprise is a pizza?' was her response. How ungrateful!

'A candlelit dinner for two!' I turned to the boy. 'How much, buddy?' I turned back to the lovely lady. 'Oh, you wouldn't mind lighting the candles would you? I'm not fire retardant.' She rolled her eyes, damn her! 'Woops, I can't find my wallet,' I said innocently. Smooth, eh?

'Look, I haven't got all night. I've got a big pizza order to deliver to some Kennedy bloke before half-past,' chirped up the insolent pizza delivery boy.

'Kennedy? To his house? But, he's only through there in his office!'

'So you see,' Mr Monkey explained, 'it all kinda fell into place.'

'So it did,' Gerty replied, sipping on her ice cold orange juice. 'Ah well, I suppose we'd better do the deed - get it over with.'

'I suppose we'd better.'

They got up and went back into the camper, where Kennedy was dangling by his arms from the ceiling.

'I'm very sorry, Inspector,' Gerty sighed, 'I take absolutely no pleasure whatsoever in torturing and killing you, but you're a very bad man and you deserve it.' She burst into tears as she picked up a big knife. 'I think this was about the size you used to kill poor innocent Craig Thompson all those years ago, wasn't it?' she asked him.

'You fucking bitch,' was his only response.

'So many other unsolved crimes - do you wish to confess to any more before I put an end to your sorry existence?' She wiped away her tears as he just stared at her. Mr Monkey became ever so limp and lifeless, lying flat and totally unfilled on the floor as Gerty took hold of the knife with both hands and dug it into Kennedy's chest. She left it there, coughing her head off as she stepped out of the way of all the blood.

It took Kennedy a while to die, as Gerty hadn't hit anything very critical in the stabbing. Instead, his blood drained out as he dangled there like a pig. Pigs were better than he was, though. He wasn't really worthy of being slotted into the same category as pigs. He had laughed like pigs laugh, and frolicked around in filth like they do. But, most of all he had oddly associated himself with a cat. Clearly he was crackers, and this is what Gerty now thought about. Surely she had done good? She realised she hadn't really done good at all. She was as bad as Kennedy now. Still, as she tried to clear her throat she knew her own time was nearing. Her dear Raymond's troubles had started with a cough. They were both heavy smokers, and in a way she always knew this day was coming. Short of breath, she let the deck chair take her weight as she summoned the strength to dispose of Kennedy's body.

For the first time in her life, Gerty was actually in need of the wheelchair that now housed her. She turned and looked down the aisle of the church as Katie entered, the wedding march playing as everyone got to their feet for the bride. She stepped nervously towards Alex at the altar in her perfect white dress, helped along by Arthur, as Ruby mopped away a tear and Emma gave a little wink. But, Gerty had already had enough and just wanted to get out of there.

A lot of booze and jigging around later, the day had come to an end and it was time for Alex to carry his bride over the threshold. He was a bit too tipsy for that, however, and the newly married pair stumbled into the wedding suite in the hotel. Katie collapsed onto the four-poster bed and found her tight hair almost melting into the feather pillow. It felt too tight, all the pins holding it off her heavily made-up face. It all felt false somehow, just a big show for everyone else. Nonetheless, at this precise moment in time she felt she did love Alex and he came next to her on the bed, lying flat out as well. They were both so exhausted after their full day performance. Things had been good between them. Well, as good as things could be. Every couple had their issues and their ups and downs.

'Shall we, you know, do it then?' Alex whispered to her. She replied with a snore. Suddenly restless, he got up and paced about the room. His phone buzzed in his pocket and he got it out. It was a text message from Emma: "You both looked so wonderful together today. So happy for you x". He knew which room Emma was in - alone - and suddenly wanted to see her. He slipped out of the room and into the corridor, where the door across from him opened. The room was dark, a woman's hand appearing from the side of the door and beckoning him in. He quickly obliged, stepping inside as the door closed.

'Hello, Alex. Congratulations,' a familiar voice spoke. It wasn't Emma - it was Michelle.

'No!' Alex replied in shock, his eyes trying to adjust to the dark.

'Yup, I got released a few days ago. I'm free,' said the blonde beauty who had spent the last decade locked up for murder.

'What are you doing here?'

'I just want to apologise for trying to kill you all those years ago.'

'You're a nutter, I'm out of here.' He grabbed hold of the door handle, but she threw her weight against it to stop him.

Suddenly a vision flashed into his mind. He could see himself, dead on this very hotel bedroom floor where he presently stood, with Michelle stepping over his corpse and heading out towards Katie. Next, Katie herself was being hacked to bits by the mad woman. Alex felt he had been delivered this future sight in order to halt its occurrence, and now found himself grabbing hold of Michelle's head and thrashing it against the wall. Taken by surprise, she fell to the floor. Quickly, Alex dived for a bedside lamp and tore it from the socket, stretching the cord around Michelle's neck and twisting it together at breakneck speed. She lashed out, trying desperately to scratch and punch him as he garrotted her. But, her efforts were to no avail as she slipped into unconsciousness and he finished her off. When he was done, and feeling surprisingly calm, he stood up from the body and waggled his fingers about to ease the sensation of pins and needles that had befallen them.

Somebody cleared their throat, and Alex put the light on. There, sitting in an armchair in the room, was Reaping Icon. 'Welcome, impressionable young man,' he said.

'Who are you?' asked Alex.

'I am you, and you are me,' he replied, looking right into Alex - into himself. 'Does The Space show you things often?'

'The Space? Why are you even asking me that? If you're me, surely you know the answer?'

'I'm terribly sorry, Alex, but there's no going back now.' Reaping Icon remained sitting, but Alex somehow sensed him right up close. 'Our immediate problem is what to do with the body.' Alex looked down at Michelle and suddenly backed away, the realisation of his actions starting to seize him. He tried to force his fist into his mouth, biting down on his knuckles as he trembled. The sweat poured off him, his hair becoming suddenly soaking wet. 'I suggest you look in that bag over there,' Reaping Icon told him, pointing at a small leather handbag on the bed.

'But, but,' Alex stuttered, blood weeping from his knuckle. 'Open the bag.'

Alex did so, finding a hacksaw and a roll of black bin bags.

'Oh God,' he spluttered, taking hold of the saw and turning to look back at Michelle.

'It's not rocket science. You either dispose of the body, or you spoil your wedding night.'

Alex dragged Michelle into the bathroom, stepping back out of it as he turned the light on in there. He looked back at the body, wiping the sweat off his forehead. He felt soaked in his clothes, so he put the hacksaw and bags down on the bed and took his suit jacket off. The sweat was absolutely pouring off him and he knew that he was going to get his clothes really mucked up if he was going to go through with sawing Michelle up. A nod from a watchful Reaping Icon spurred him on to remove all of his clothes, which he tossed on the bed. He now stood, stark naked, and looked at Reaping Icon.

'I can't do this,' he moaned.

'You must, for both our sakes,' Reaping Icon replied.

'Why, what have you got to lose?'

Reaping Icon looked around and behind Alex, frowning. But, Alex would not turn and look. He knew no one was there. Reluctantly, he stepped back into the bathroom with the hacksaw and bags and locked the door. There was Michelle on the floor, the cord still tight around her neck. Her face now seemed unrecognisable to Alex. Regardless, he didn't want to look at it anyway. He bent down and turned it to face the bath. Her clothing now got his attention. She was wearing a rather nice green dress, which had become somewhat creased in the struggle. Her legs were bare, and Alex touched them. They were really smooth and still warm. She'd always been one of the prettier girls in school, and Alex had often fantasised in his youth about touching her. Little did he ever imagine himself naked in a locked hotel bathroom with her - and she couldn't stop him now.

Again he thought of her dress, wishing Katie would wear something like it. It was a figure hugger, not the baggy sort of thing Katie always had on. Perhaps he could give it to his new wife as a present, he thought? Maybe she would try something like it now they were married. Besides, Michelle no longer needed it. Thus, he set about getting it off her. Firstly,he tried to pull it over her head, but the ghastly bloated navy blue tinge of her neck and cheeks waving about under him as he tried was a bit too much to cope with. His penis, too, waved about in the same scope of vision, and confused him even further about the situation. He concluded that the best way to get the dress off was to pull it down.

Dress off, and placed carefully to one side in the hope it would not get mucked up, Alex put the blade of the saw against her leg. He couldn't bear to picture what he was about to do. It absolutely horrified him. He was *SO* angry at Michelle for having done this to him. What had she done to him? She was the one who was dead, and he'd murdered her. He looked at her tight white knickers. They were wet, and he touched them out of curiosity. Surely they had to come off too - and her bra? Placing the hacksaw down, he set about removing her underwear. This made him even angrier - he wanted to thrash at her limp body to somehow get recompense for his upset night. Less and less was he thinking about what he had done to her, and more and more what he perceived she had done to him. She had denied him his wedding night shag, he came to believe.

He touched Michelle's dead vagina - still warm, and wet. The rage exploded inside him, and he pulled her legs apart and knelt down in between them. His flaccid penis stayed curled up like a dead gerbil as he struggled to blank from his mind what he was doing. Straightening his penis out, he felt for Michelle's vagina with its tip. Suddenly her head turned to face him, her eyes opening to catch sight of what was happening above her. Flabbergasted that she was actually still alive, Alex froze in position. Finding her hands immediately around his neck, and her legs wrapped around his, he became erect and forced himself into her. His entire being throbbed like never before, his penis numbing as Michelle squeezed tighter and tighter around his neck. Her legs now stretched up onto his bum, almost like she was encouraging and even aiding his thrusts. The sweat poured off the pair, Alex's sticky body collapsing onto hers as he passed out. She kept on squeezing around his neck as she found her own breaths difficult to take with his weight now crushing her. Eventually slithering from underneath the man, she clamoured for the sink and pulled herself up. She rubbed at her pounding head, catching sight of herself in the bathroom mirror. It was now that she undid the cord around her neck, lost in her own reflection. It wasn't her looking back - it was this half dead thing she couldn't place at all. She was right back in the same mindset she'd been in all those years ago in the hospital when she'd tried to finish Alex off. Katie had been bashing on the window, trying desperately to get in and save her Alex. Katie! She was just across the corridor, ready for the slaughter in her white dress. Would Alex be able to come to her rescue? Michelle wasn't going to give him the option.

She quickly tied the cord around his neck, pulling him up with all her strength and propping him against the bath as she got her shoulders under his arms and wrestled with his weight to get him to stand. With enough length of the cord, she managed to stretch it over the shower curtain rail and wrapped it around, keeping hold of it as she let Alex go. His dead weight pulled him down as she tugged mightily at the cord, tying a loose knot in it to keep him there. Picking the hacksaw up, she glanced down at his exposed penis. She'd have sawn it off, but didn't much fancy touching it.

Katie was sleeping when Michelle crept into the room, but stirred as her imminent killer approached. Just about making out a naked female figure in the near total darkness, Katie seemed joyed. 'You managed to get rid of Alex then?' she whispered seductively. Michelle did not reply as Katie pulled her wedding dress up and slipped her knickers off. She tossed them carelessly onto the floor and lay back on the bed. 'Eat me, Emma, consume all of me.' This stopped Michelle in her tracks. She placed the hacksaw down on the bedside cabinet and knelt on the bed. Katie's hand felt blindly in the dark, meeting with Michelle's vagina in front. She rubbed her finger up and down it, which did not displease its owner. 'Wow, you're so wet for me,' Katie continued, playing with her clitoris with her free hand. Michelle hesitated for but a moment, before reaching out and feeling her way around Katie's legs. She lay herself down, half on the bed and half off the end, burying her head in between Katie's legs and licking furiously at the sopping pussy. Katie's buttocks clenched as Michelle grabbed hold of them and pulled her closer. Their whole beings, entangled in this brief flash of ecstasy, soared together as a singular beast intent on delirious pleasure. Michelle gobbled quicker and quicker, pulling at the lips with her teeth and penetrating with her tongue. Katie was completely lost in the sensation, and yet was more in her own body than ever before. She completely let go, screaming out as she felt herself spinning uncontrollably around the room.

All of a sudden the light was on and Katie, startled, screwed her eyes up. The pleasure stopped and, when she opened her eyes again, Alex and Michelle were grappling with the hacksaw. Katie recognised Michelle and was horrified. All that she had just been through was with *HER* and not Emma. Did it really matter, though? Alex seemed to get the upper hand in the fight and Michelle was thrown face-first at the window, which shattered. Shards of glass now protruding from her eyes and cheeks, she waved desperately about the room with the hacksaw, catching Alex's arm. One last stumble back saw her slip out of the window. Alex rushed to it, just in time to see Michelle lying in a mess outside on the ground so far below. He looked back at his wife, her wedding dress all ruffled up by her waist and her legs spread wide open. It was the first time he'd seen her bits in the light.

The whole day had taken its toll on Gerty's already weak body, and all she wanted to do was sleep. Here she lay, in her own bed in her house in Myrtle Mews, thinking of her dear late husband Raymond. There were no sad thoughts - she just wanted to be with him again. It had always just been the two of them. Years and years and years they had gone about things together, including their favourite hobby: smoking. Still, Gerty wasn't too bothered - something had to get you in the end. She'd led a pretty charmed life, really, and gotten away with quite a few crimes. Her only regret was that she never had managed to take Raymond's ashes to Harnlan. Always sidetracked, she had gotten carried away with one thing and another and never got around to it. Still, in a way she was glad. His urn was next to her right now, and she sensed he was close to her.

'Look at me, Mr Monkey, I'm hideous,' she said to her ever faithful puppet companion as he appeared by her bedside. She pulled her wig off, revealing the extent of her illness. Her emaciated face now seemed right, though, as the wig had been too extravagant.

'I think you're beautiful, Mrs Hinklebottom,' he replied.

'Please, call me Gerty.'

She did have Mr Monkey, at least. But, he was no replacement for Raymond. Perhaps Mr Monkey would do her the same favour as she had done for Raymond and her mother? No, she thought, that had hardly been a favour. Her memories of her beloved husband and mother had been marred by the moments replayed in her mind every day since their demise - demises she brought about at their requests. She would not burden Mr Monkey with that, even if he was just a puppet. Equally, she felt she had not been burdened at all. She just couldn't decide. Either way, nature decided for her and she felt her heart stopping. There was that split second realisation that she was a goner, before it was actually reality for the sole onlooker of the event: Mr Monkey. A tear rolled from one of his purple button eyes and down his cheek, soaking into his polyester fur.